Dedicated to my favourite star.
You know who you are!

Chapter One

On a sun scorched street on the Costa del Sol, a small group of tourists sat lazily on wicker loungers outside a beachside bar and cheered raucously as the waiter set their eighth jug of Sangria on the table. It was Sunday. They had gone to the beach that morning to nurse their collective hangovers, and by early afternoon they had moved on to the protective shade of the nearby *Straw Donkey* bar, to ease their blistering sunburn, where they got an early start working on the next day's inevitable hangover. The equally hung-over waiter's blank responses indicated that he didn't speak any English, but after some creative pointing and shouting the group had managed to order the cheapest, largest drink on the menu, and left the lone server to continue watching some strange Spanish reality television show that was apparently enthralling him.

A copy of *Celebs Today*, a notoriously scandalous British tabloid magazine that one of the women had picked up in a local store, was prompting an energetic discussion that engaged the intoxicated holidaymakers.

"Phwoar, look at that one!"
"Come on, her tits are as fake as a nine bob note!"
"No way!"
"You can see the scars! Her nipples are practically pointing up 'er nose!"

The Sangria was eagerly shared out among them and the youngest of the men gestured immediately at the waiter for another jug, eager to impress his new girlfriend with his legendary wit and charm that he felt definitely improved with every glass he knocked back. The conversation grew livelier and the pages turned faster as the ruthless celebrity scrutiny intensified.

"I reckon she's only with him for the money".
"You just know *she* didn't actually pay six grand for that designer handbag, though".
"Hasn't *he* aged badly? He'd need to spill a drink on my lap to get me wet these days!"
"Look at those duck lips! So obviously fake! No way she had them before!"
"Grubby fingernails, though! I'm guessing that *soap* isn't her favourite four letter word!"
"Urgh, I hate this actor. I'd like to just slap him in the face... only with my car!"
"Do you reckon it's true he was having an affair?"
"Probably just to make her jealous. It's always a tit-for-tat power struggle with those posh types".
"I bet all these celeb men cheat anyway. Stands to reason, all these gorgeous girls throwing themselves at them".
"Well they all get caught eventually. Look at that Roger Scott guy a few months back".
"Never heard of him!"
"Yeah, he used to be a footballer. Had a lot of promise 'til the scandal. I actually felt quite sorry for him, well, until

it turned out that he'd also been shaggin' all those birds behind his wife's back, of course. Smug git!"

"Can't – *hiccup* - blame him, actually". This response from the youngest man of the party earned him yet another dangerously icy glare from his new girlfriend that didn't escape his attention this time. He tactically turned the page. It was time to turn up the infallible charm, he decided. It was another poor celebrity's turn to face their unforgiving observations…

"Hey, look at her! She's had more – *hiccup* – than a used dartboard, that one!"

Suddenly deciding she was bored of this celebrity social commentary, the unfortunate man's now soon-to-be-ex-girlfriend glanced moodily around the seafront and noticed another cheap rental car speedily pull up in the street. This wasn't a particularly nice or popular beach even at the peak of summer, in spite of what the group's tour operator had promised them, so there weren't many people around to look at. Most of the little stores around them had closed for the afternoon 'siesta' and there didn't seem to be anybody else around this unfashionable end of town today, except for one odd looking chap who had been lingering for some time across the street with a long lensed camera hanging from around his neck and an impatient look on his face. He was still there. *'Probably just some pervert'*, she casually dismissed without any apparent alarm as she let her attention drift idly back to the rental car.

She observed a lone woman in an ill-fitting sarong climb gracelessly out of the driver's seat and remove her ridiculously oversized sunglasses. The new visitor did look strangely familiar, somehow.

Suddenly, a penny dropped in the tourist's Sangria-frazzled mind. "Hey!" she loudly announced, turning back to her friends in excitement. "Look! Look over there! Isn't that old *whatsherface*? Y'know... from that reality show a while back! It *is*! Over there – it's *Lottie Klünt!*"

Lottie Klünt ambled out of her car and hoped that she had finally found the right beach. She had struggled all afternoon with a rental car more erratic than *Herbie* and a GPS system that seemed not to recognise any highway, street or building built after 1982, but after three false starts she had finally reached her intended destination. She would have to be quick and just hope that she wasn't too late.

Muttering and cursing under her breath, she clumsily jiggled and fought her way out of the itchy sarong that had been two sizes too small for her when she had bought it. It was at least four sizes too small now and was dangerously close to becoming part of her permanent anatomy. After eventually freeing herself from the stifling garment with an irritable grunt, she allowed herself a discreet glance at her surroundings and pretended not to notice the impatient lone photographer who was still standing facing the deserted beach.

Genuinely oblivious to the nosy group of tourists watching her from the bar, Lottie Klünt threw her long-suffering sarong, oversized sunhat and sweaty t-shirt onto the backseat of the car and began walking alone down the empty beach towards the ocean. As she reached the halfway point, she stopped and fumbled unnecessarily with her mismatched bikini, exposing one half of her wobbly backside and allowing a strap from her bikini top to hang precociously off her shoulder. It was horribly unflattering. Even the tourists at the bar, who normally considered uncomplimentary pictures of minor celebrities to be the height of cultural entertainment, had fallen into a stunned silence at the undignified sight in front of them.

'Does she not realise how bad she looks?' they asked themselves, unable to take their eyes off the fallen D-lister.

After a few minutes of unsexy posing on the beach, Lottie Klünt lumbered inelegantly into the sea and began to splash around in an odd manner, laughing wildly to herself in fake delight despite there being no one else around. For no obvious reason, she then appeared to subject her painfully overstretched bikini top to a swift forceful tug and – like watching an overburdened shelf collapse under its own weight – one of her breasts made a predictable bid for freedom, and flopped out in an asymmetrical crude display of overexposure.

Lottie gasped and covered the offending nipple with her hand to preserve her non-existent modesty, but then – to the bafflement of the *Straw Donkey*'s drunken patrons, their waiter and even a couple of passersby whose attention had been roused by Lottie's curious display - she repeated the action twice more, each time expressing great astonishment and embarrassment at her own voluptuous 'nip slip' as though she didn't know it was coming!

Unnoticed by everyone except Lottie, the lone photographer across the street eventually gave a subtle thumbs-up gesture and swiftly disappeared.
Thirty seconds later, Lottie left the beach, jumped back into her rental car and left her bewildered audience to continue with their lives.

"*What the hell was that about?*" the waiter asked in confusion, inadvertently revealing his perfect spoken English to his puzzled customers.

....

David Paige arrived thirty minutes early at the offices of *Tomorrow First* magazine and tried hard to suppress his evident irritability before his job interview. He had spent the morning at his own office at *Celebs Today* magazine reading through angry threats of lawsuits from slighted stars, desperate pleas for exposure from wannabe celebs and an even angrier tirade from his obnoxious boss who was unhappy with their recent sales and apparently wanted *better* real life events to report on. While this was nothing new, it had done nothing to benefit David's temperament and he could feel the enthusiastic, dynamic and ambitious impression he had wanted to make in his interview being replaced by one that was sullen, grumpy and defensive.

"Find better gossip!" David's boss had screamed at him after the disappointing weekly sales figures had arrived that morning. "I'm fed up of the same do-nothing bimbos, dead-end relationships and yo-yo dieters every soddin' week! Can't something actually *happen* for once?!"

Ashton Cain had been the Editor-in-Chief – the tabloid's highest job position - at *Celebs Today* for just less than a year, much to the incomprehension and resentment of David, who was currently the magazine's long-standing, long-suffering Executive Editor and had always considered himself to be far more qualified for the coveted chief role. It was unfair, David considered repeatedly, but it was just one of many injustices that he had observed all his life. People just didn't seem to warm to him. He didn't know what it was. Perhaps he had spent too long working in the murky world of low rent celebrity journalism, but somewhere along the way he had developed a love/hate relationship with humanity and mostly saw the ugliness in people, and how this could be best exploited.

The feeling, humanity seemed to be telling him, *was entirely mutual.*

David had spent more than a decade working for *Celebs Today* and had entered the job, as far as he could remember, as an enthusiastic newlywed with high hopes, an ambitious attitude and a thirst for exciting investigative journalism in the glamorous world of showbiz. It hadn't taken him particularly far. Ashton Cain, by contrast, had seemingly walked into the offices practically straight out of preschool, charmed a few influential people and stabbed everybody else in the back in a remorseless sort of way, and had been rewarded with the magazine's highest job position, an undeservingly high salary and an eye-wateringly large expense account on top. It just seemed so unfair.

'What could that obnoxious snot-faced pretty boy possibly have that I don't?' David had internally asked himself with bitterness almost every day since.

David's wife Angelica – his now-*estranged* wife, he mentally reminded himself – had always accused him of being passive-aggressive. This was absolutely true. It was one of the few things they could have actually agreed on, except that David would never have admitted to this and continued to disagree with her anyway because a man has to have his principles.

The problem was that being passive-aggressive was the only way David knew how to be, so whenever he tried to fight against this natural default behaviour, he would either end up simply behaving passively *or* aggressively with no apparent middle ground whatsoever.

Recognising this, he had long ago decided to do the best he could within the confines of this limited personality repertoire, submerged himself into his career and decided not to be burdened with a desire to change or improve himself.
It had been going somewhat smoothly for David, until his wife had one day decided that after ten years of marriage she suddenly hated everything about him except for his credit cards, and the one man who could put David in a worse mood than an alcoholic during prohibition had been unfairly hired above him.
David wasn't the type of person to stab somebody in the back, but he was growing tired of being overlooked and underestimated. He was becoming fed up of being overworked and undermined. He definitely was sick of

being perpetually at the back of the queue in life.

After forty-five minutes of waiting and trying hard not to be annoyed about it, David heard the office door open as another candidate's interview had finally come to an end. Discreetly peering around the water cooler that was inconveniently blocking his view, he saw a well-dressed, good looking man about half David's age emerge from the interviewer's office, laughing and smiling as he shook the interviewer's hand. As the man walked confidently into the reception area, he called out the receptionist's name and thanked her personally, while David cursed himself for not bothering to do the same. The clearly smitten woman heartily wished the handsome interviewee good luck, sat back in her chair and then completely forgot all about David despite there being no-one else waiting.

He cleared his throat. She didn't notice.
He cleared his throat again. Again, she entirely failed to notice.

This unreciprocated signalling lasted for a full four minutes before the receptionist remembered David, and distractedly directed him to the office to finally begin his job interview.

"Hmm", the interviewer repeated unenthusiastically as he read through David's qualifications and job history in front of him a few minutes later. This part should have been easy. David knew that he was more than qualified for the position he was applying for but for some reason the interviewer looked uncertain at what he was reading, and it was becoming disconcerting the way the man continued to make no sound except for his repeated, grating hum of indifference.

"Well, I can see that you're experienced, Mr Paige. My concern is that *Celebs Today*... Well, it's all a bit *yesterday*, isn't it?" the interviewer eventually spoke, making a well-meaning but unsuccessful effort to sound empathetic. "I sometimes read your mag on my short commute to work. Half of the sources you refer to in your stories are actually your rival magazines who'd already reported the same story days before! I know it's not your fault specifically, but I'm concerned that someone who's spent so long working in such a small pond might not be the big fish we're looking for here at *Tomorrow First*".

David left the interview a few minutes later feeling dejected. He did *not* thank the receptionist.

Predictably, she completely failed to notice.

....

Renowned PR guru Clive Maxwell sat facing his client and paused wearily for a moment. He had been a public relations specialist for many gruelling decades and had long ago learned to recognise the blank, vacant stare of the perpetually absent-minded that gazed back at him. He had spent more than enough time in the company of these flash-in-a-pan celebs desperate to extend their fifteen minutes of fame to know that they generally had the attention span of a gnat, and he tried to remind himself that he was an unjustly expensive PR leader who still charged by the hour.

Their notoriously non-existent attention span might be frustrating at times, but people like Clive had certainly found that it could be very profitable.

His client waited expectantly in dead-eyed silence, seemingly without a single thought in his beautifully sculpted head, and Clive wondered for a moment just how long the man would actually wait for if left unprompted. It occurred to Clive, not for the first time, that many of his clients resembled nothing more than cute wooden puppets whose puppeteer had gone outside for an extended cigarette break. It suited him just fine. Nobody with an IQ above room temperature would be willing to pay what he charged for his services, and thankfully he knew this better than anyone.

Clive drummed his fingers on the desk thoughtfully. He cleared his throat as though contemplating something important. He picked up one of the tabloid magazines in front of him and stared at it quizzically. Finally, he heard the subtle satisfying click of the wall clock indicate that it was now two o'clock and made a mental note to invoice his client for another hour, taking the all-too-common view that even a minute past the hour technically could be billed as another full hour's work.

"Okay Roger. *This* is what we're going to do", Clive began as he prepared to repeat everything he had been saying for the past few weeks, "Obviously, we have to accept that no reputable football club is going to hire you so soon after your hit and run scandal, which brings me to my first point... *No* more drinking and driving!"
Roger gave a vague shrug of acknowledgement. Clive continued, "But that doesn't mean that your public image can't recover. The world of showbiz is far more forgiving, and frankly I've had lesser celebs commit bigger crimes than yours in this very office! But I digress... Our bigger problem now is that your profile took a massive hit with the recent cheating scandal. The general public didn't like that one bit! Your loyal wife Cherlene stands by you throughout your prison stint and failed career, and you get caught with your pants down – if you'll pardon the pun – *roger-ing* some high-class escort who sold every sleazy detail of it to the press".

Clive paused expectantly. Disappointingly, his little pun had failed to register with his client. *'Probably not lowbrow enough'*, Clive thought to himself.

15

He continued unabated, "What we need to do now is reinvent you as a reformed character, a loving husband who has moved on from his past indiscretions. We need to see pictures of you holding your wife's coat, buying her jewellery, supporting her endeavours and so on. We need to see you committing your time to charities, working with kids. Animals, too! That's always a good one! We'll show your humble side a bit more – paparazzi photos of you walking the dog, washing the car and so on. Well, maybe not the car specifically, but you get the general idea. People love that stuff. What we *don't* need to see is another bloody 'Roger Scott Cheats On His Wife' headline! Understood?"

Roger agreed, thanked his agent, picked up his rucksack and, after pausing unnecessarily to admire his handsome reflection in the mirror, made his way out of the office. He had always liked Clive and respected his opinion. The man was *smart*. He buried scandals easier than dogs buried bones, and he knew how to play the fame game better than anybody else, at least according to his reputation. Roger trusted his PR agent explicitly, and he looked forward to his public reinvention as a loving and devoted husband.

Roger walked to the reception area and checked that he had a taxi waiting for him outside. He did. He checked with the receptionist that the fire alarms had been deactivated so that he could sneak inconspicuously out of the side door. They had. He then reached into his rucksack and took out a small wig, a pair of sunglasses, an oversized coat and a large red baseball cap. As he put them on, he thought longingly of the escort he had hired for the afternoon, and wondered if she would already be waiting for him when he arrived at the apartment that he had secretly rented for his extra marital liaisons.

Once he was satisfied with his ridiculous disguise, Roger thanked the receptionist and approached the fire exit. Just as he was about to push open the door, he remembered one last little detail and took out his phone.

"Hi Cherlene, it's me. I'm sorry babe, but the meeting with Clive is going to take a bit longer than I thought. I'll just be another couple of hours and then I'll see you for dinner".

"No worries, sweetie", his wife skilfully lied with an impenetrably sweet and loving tone, "I've got my book club this afternoon anyway. You take your time and I'll see you when you get home".

Poor Roger, Cherlene thought to herself as she left the house a few minutes later. *He's always so preoccupied with telling his own lies, that he never bothers to even consider that other people might be lying to him too!*

This would ultimately prove to be a rather important lesson that Roger would learn sooner than later, and the cost of this unexpected lesson would be life-changing. But he had no way of knowing this yet.

For if ignorance truly is bliss in life, then Roger Scott's life was practically orgasmic.

Chapter Two

Former reality TV star Lottie Klünt parked in the centre of town and as she stepped out of her rental car, she was greeted with a rousing chorus of car horns and general jeering. *'Wow, I must be more famous here than I am in Britain!'* she thought to herself proudly, as she tried to portray a demure look and waved graciously at the excited townsfolk. An elderly woman emerged from a nearby store and quickly approached her.

"*¡No puedes aparcar aqui!*" the old woman shrilled animatedly.
"Oh, erm. I don't speak foreign", Lottie apologised. "I guess you guys get the British tabloids here. *Do – You – Want – An – Autograph?*" she added patronisingly, making a pen and paper motion with her hands. To Lottie's bafflement, the ancient woman groaned and threw her hands up in the air derisively.
"*English?*" she bellowed with a heavy accent, "You may not park your car here!"

With sudden red-faced awareness, Lottie finally noticed the traffic standstill she had inadvertently caused with her illegal parking and all the angry faces that were shouting at her to move. She finally realised that nobody had recognised her after all, and for a moment, possibly for the first time in her entire life, she was genuinely grateful for this.

Humiliated and dejected, she ignored the old crone who was still shrieking at her in Spanish, and jumped back into her wretched rental car.

"Bitch!" she muttered under her breath as she sped away.

"¡Puta!" the old woman muttered as she returned to her store.

Twenty minutes later, Lottie thundered breathlessly into a small quiet café and found the paparazzi photographer from the beach sitting alone at a table. He looked even more impatient than before.

"It's about time! I bet even Mariah bleedin' Carey doesn't keep people waiting for *this* long", he scolded her, grumpily.

"Sorry!" she gasped, trying to catch her breath. "You can't park anywhere in this town! I had to ditch the car and run here! I think that this sarong is actually cutting off my blood circulation!"

"No kidding!" the pap replied with a cruel laugh. He felt much happier now that he knew the woman who had been keeping him waiting all day was at least suffering for it.

"Well I've got some good shots today", he went on with sudden sadistic cheerfulness, "My word, you've gotten really fat, haven't you? I remember all those sexy lingerie photos you did after you left that reality TV show a couple of years back. You must be twice the size now!"

With a swift indignant huff, Lottie shoved the dessert menu she had been idly glancing at back into its little plastic stand.

"Don't worry about it", the photographer laughed in an amused tone that Lottie found somehow more irritating than his grumpy one. "People lost interest in you long ago, but they always love to see photos of a formerly hot celeb who's piled on the pounds. It's the next best thing to a plastic surgery disaster, although I still wouldn't rule that out if I were you".

Lottie smiled uncertainly. She liked being described as a "hot celeb". She just hated that it was only ever used in the past tense to describe her now. Still, if a few unflattering holiday photos of her were all it would take to keep her in the spotlight, then she could suffer the indignity of them for now at least. She knew with absolute conviction that if she could just keep the momentum of her tenuous notoriety going for a bit longer, then she could capitalise on it with all kinds of new ventures. She could always lose the weight afterwards. She might even get one of those lucrative celebrity fitness video deals or something.

"Just a little friendly advice, though", the photographer added as he fiddled with his camera and scrolled through the unsightly beach pictures. "The photo agency will probably find a buyer for these photos today, but these *'let's-all-laugh-at-Lottie's-weight-gain pics'* aren't really fetching as much money as they used to. To put it frankly, your fat arse might be able to cause a mini-tsunami when you're flopping about in the Mediterranean Sea pretending to be on holiday for a few staged pap shots, but you're not exactly making waves anymore as far as the press is concerned. Haven't you got anything else to fall back on?"

Lottie didn't.

"Well I suggest you come up with *something*", he went on, thinking aloud. "Even a scandal is better than nothing, but you can only plunge so far into obscurity before there's no coming back".

As Lottie absorbed this ominous warning about her rapidly expiring fifteen minutes of fame, the photographer – who was never very good at sensing when he should stop thinking aloud - needlessly concluded, "After all, talentless fame whores normally get by on their good looks, but I didn't need a long lensed camera to see that *that* bus has long since departed!"

David returned to his office at *Celebs Today* later that afternoon, still feeling despondent about his dismal job interview earlier in the day. He already knew with every cynical, miserable fibre of his being that his mood wasn't going to improve today and felt something akin to a small scrap of satisfaction when his assistant seemingly confirmed this, as he greeted David with a couple of messages from his estranged wife, Angelica. The first message was to announce that she had rescheduled their planned marriage counselling session again for absolutely no good reason whatsoever, and the second message was just a list of social functions that she was planning to attend over the next few weeks with a strong warning that David should not plan on being at the same place at the same time as her. They had only been separated for just less than six weeks, but already her social life was seemingly embracing a comeback more impressive than Robert Downey Junior's film career.

David took an angry look at the list. "She doesn't want me to attend Jim and Gerry's wedding? I *introduced* them!" he ranted to no one in particular. "She's already got the house that *I* paid for, and now my succubus bride is taking possession of my friends, too? What next? We're supposed to be fixing our marriage, not dividing our assets! Or at least that's what the witch told me when she kicked me out. I should probably count my blessings that the old cow is so bloody work-shy or she'd be demanding my job too!"

David put down the list and looked around him. Nobody was paying him any attention at all. His assistant was chatting casually on the phone, and everybody else was simply ignoring David in an unaffected, obvious sort of way. He almost appreciated the honesty.

"Ashton has somebody waiting for you in your office", David's assistant said as he put down the phone. "Mrs Cherlene Scott apparently arrived earlier to discuss doing some features with the magazine or something. Ashton was vague on the details but he's assigned the task to you. I don't think he really knows what she wants, to be honest. Oh, Cherlene – that's the footballer *Roger Scott*'s wife, if you didn't recognise the name".

David thanked him grumpily and made a vague attempt at a polite smile. He was feeling grouchy but always made a point not to be unkind. Back-stabbers like Ashton Cain were unkind, not people like David, who more often than not felt as though he was the one being stabbed.
'I'm the Executive Editor and I get stuck meeting some ex-footballer's wife who probably wants to talk about her latest perm', David grumbled under his breath as he stomped towards his office. *'I almost wish that Angelica did want to take my job in the separation after all!"*

24

"Cherlene Scott, how *lovely* to see you! You look fantastic!" David chirped in the friendliest voice he could muster up as he entered his office. Cherlene was already sitting at his desk, waiting and fiddling with her enormous engagement ring and wedding band. He breezily went on, "I think we've met once already, at a charity luncheon. Weren't we raising awareness about starving kids or starving animals... or starving something? I can't recall. The buffet was good, though, whatever it was for! And the champagne! Do you remember?"

"Roger's cheatin' on me again", she blurted out, abruptly disregarding David's genuine attempt at friendliness. "I hired a private detective. Look, I've got all these pictures of him meeting other women at his secret apartment that he thinks I don't know about. He's wearing some stupid wig but you can tell it's him. They're all dated within the last few weeks, too".

She placed more than a dozen photos on David's desk and continued, "Some of 'em are escorts, but not all of 'em. Look, one of the women even has a wedding ring on! The cheek of it!"

David ignored the photo and opened his mouth to say something comforting, but was instantly cut off before he could speak. Cherlene clearly hadn't reached her main point yet.

"I haven't told my agent about this, because he's Roger's agent too and I don't want him to know yet. *Nobody knows about this. Nobody at all.* Well, except for the detective. Oh, and you know now, I guess. Anyway, this is the *end* for me and Roger. And I want *you* to make me famous!"

David opened his mouth again but this time found no words.

Cherlene continued more passionately, "He's betrayed me too many times this time. Do you think I don't know how *hot* I am? I've turned down all kinds of photo shoots and TV appearances 'cause I wanted to be all loyal and let him be the big celebrity without his wife upstaging him or whatever. Well no more! I want to do a big tell-all interview when I announce the divorce. I want to really shame him! I want to do a big sexy photo shoot for it, too. I'll tell you everything you want to know about him. Well, not *everything*. I'm trying to get one of those ghost-written autobiography deals, so I'll have to save a little something about Roger for that, 'cause I haven't really done anything else except marrying him if I'm honest and the publishers have already said I'm not really famous enough yet to do a book about. The interview'll quickly change that, though! Do you mind if I make some of it up?"

"Well, there's certainly a *very* fine line in the media between telling your version of the truth that you want to tell, and telling an outright lie that you can be caught out in", David responded as he quickly caught up with the situation. "I'll put you in contact with our legal department who can best advise you when it comes to these specifics, and it might be an idea that you give me the contact info of the private detective you hired, just in case we need to confirm any of the details".

David stared at Cherlene while she gazed out of the window, deep in thought. It occurred to him that she really *was* "hot", even if it had sounded a little conceited to hear her describe herself in such a way. *'What on earth was Roger thinking?'* he privately wondered. David picked up the incriminating photos of Roger with his various lovers and began idly flicking through them. It was weird. None of the women Roger had chosen to commit his extra marital affairs with could hold a candle to Cherlene, as far as David could judge. Curiously, one of the pictures in particular then caught his eye.

"You know, I really thought that marriage was forever", Cherlene sighed woefully. "I *loved* being a footballer's wife in the beginning. It just seemed so glamorous and romantic. I genuinely never thought it would come to this, not even after the first time I caught him cheating. But there's only so much you can put up with before something snaps. Do you know what I mean, David? I guess I'll have to accept that I'll soon be back on the singles' market again..."

"Hmm? Oh, yes. Yes, I suppose you will", David responded, still firmly transfixed on the particular photo he was clutching of Roger kissing one of his lovers. He had just at that moment decided, once and for all, exactly what he was going to do about his troubled marriage. He was going to finally ask for a divorce! He already knew how his wife would react but he reached the conclusion then and there that he simply didn't care anymore. Cherlene was right. Something had finally snapped.

Angelica would probably be delighted to hear the news, but David decided to do it anyway.

Chapter Three

Former reality TV star Lottie was relieved to be able to return to London after spending two days ambling around the Costa del Sol, pretending to be on holiday and engaging in the degrading public theatrics for the benefit of the pre-arranged paparazzi photographer. She knew that some of the photos would be picked up and published by at least one of the tabloids – all the weight she had gained lately would ensure that – but she could never escape the feeling that there was something crass and faintly sordid about participating in these staged 'pap pics'. Naturally, part of her enjoyed the easy money that could be made from them, and Lottie had happily become accustomed to feeling like the centre of attention over the years, but she still couldn't help but hate the fact that the tabloids and its readership were apparently only interested in seeing photos of her as long as they were humiliating photos that they could all laugh and scoff at. It was almost difficult to remember or even explain what all the effort was actually for, once you really thought about it. Lottie had always tried to make the best of her position. She really had. She had always been aware that fame was a fleeting concept, even back in the beginning, and that it was something that so few of the people who sought it ever managed to achieve to any meaningful extent. So, she had tried to justify her position by throwing her support behind some of the more popular charity causes throughout her time in the spotlight. She had tried spirituality, that is to say that she had at least tried those that had been fashionable at the time. Lottie's initial legitimate enthusiasm for each of these fads hadn't really lasted for much more than the first fifteen minutes, but she had tried to make a difference. She had genuinely tried to supplement some kind of deeper meaning to her somewhat disingenuous fame and fortune, at least in the early days. She had even tried some expensive therapies in a bid to find her 'inner self', and only gave up when she began to suspect that she didn't actually have one.

Nobody ever seemed to want to see a 'Lottie Klünt Looks Happy' article or a 'Lottie Klünt Achieves Something' headline. No, they weren't remotely interested unless she was vomiting on her shoes, having so-called makeup disasters or being caught doing something disgraceful. It wasn't a massive distinction. Lottie had definitely proved herself to be a more than willing participant in the fame game ever since she had first gained instant notoriety on a once-popular reality TV show a few short years ago. Once she had experienced even a taste of the adoration, recognition and expensive freebies that traditionally came with being a household name, she had simply found it too hard to give up. There was just an almost indistinguishable line between being *recognised* by the public and being *liked* by them, and it occasionally bothered Lottie as she wondered which side of the coin she actually fell on.

It seemed that the public always wanted to see a car crash, but they didn't care in the slightest about the people who had taken the time to learn the skills to build the car. It could actually be quite disheartening if you allowed yourself to think about it too much. Who was it that said that 'people don't actually love celebrities; they just love to *hate* them'?

Still, it could be a lot worse. Lottie had heard some shocking stories over the past few years, and she knew that people had gone to much greater lengths in order to chase their tenuous, undeserving fame; all of them almost hypnotically led by the tantalising lure of the illustrious spotlight.

It was common knowledge that there were girls who had sought fame by accidently-on-purpose recording themselves having sex on tape, releasing the video online and then pleading innocence about the whole thing by claiming to have been betrayed or that they had been the victim of a robbery, but Lottie had known some of these girls personally and had been horrified to realise just *how* contrived these 'leaked' tapes actually were. She shuddered as she recalled an old TV acquaintance that had once explained to Lottie how her own mother had orchestrated and sold her daughter's sex-tape, just for the mere chance that her daughter could become vaguely famous for it. She knew about career-boosting sham romances. She knew of secretly gay men who had been coerced into sleeping with women they didn't even like on a personal level, women whose managers were practically more in control of their client's sex lives than the women themselves, married couples pretending that they hadn't separated, real couples pretending to still be single – the whole pursuit of fame and fortune was built on lies! Pregnancies were hidden and secret births were covered up, while others used surrogate mothers and *pretended* to be pregnant, sometimes for no better reason than to avoid the risk of ruining their marketable figures by going through the messy business of actually giving birth.

Lottie knew countless celebrities who were covering up secret drug habits. She also knew people who were simply *pretending* to be on drugs, just for the sheer attention that the rumours might bring. Classy people pretending to be *Class A* people and vice versa. Celebrities disguising and denying their cosmetic surgeries from the baying public was pretty standard business, but Lottie had at least one friend from her days in reality TV who had done exactly the opposite. The woman had, at the suggestion of her PR manager, endured unnecessary collagen injections into her lip and had even prearranged that a paparazzi photographer would 'catch' her leaving the clinic, just when she was at her most swollen and unpleasant looking. Like the modern day equivalent of somebody joining a Victorian 'freak show', she did this to her own face *knowing* full well that it would make her a laughing stock. She didn't care. She just wanted to be *seen*.

Compared to all the low-level pimping and body mutilations going on as people sought fame and fortune through any means necessary - without resorting to anything too drastic like learning a craft or skill, naturally - Lottie considered that her little prearranged public weight gain exposé barely counted. It was practically *honest*, at least by the crass standards of tenuous celebrity.

....

Celebs Today highest ranking magazine editor, David Paige, sat in unhappy silence and continued to wait for his turn to speak. He had been paying for these weekly marriage guidance sessions for exactly one month now, and coincidently he had been regretting them for exactly one month, too. His face remained a forced mask of composure and self-control as he listened intently, and he tried hard to ignore the wall clock in front of him. It hadn't escaped his attention that it had now been almost ten full minutes since he had last been permitted to speak. It had been almost ten full years since his wife had genuinely listened to anything he had to say anyway.

"And it's not just the *way* he looks at me that repulses me", Angelica continued remorselessly to the supposedly-impartial-but-blatantly-not marriage counsellor, "It's also the way he *doesn't* look at me. That makes me sick, too! I can spend hours telling him about my day, what's annoying me at that moment or what I think is generally wrong with him, and he just *sits* there with that dumb, thoughtful look on his face".

Shockingly, the counsellor seemed to agree with this outrageously unfair character assassination, and David struggled at that moment to decide which of the two women he hated more. Once a week he had to pay a small fortune for the one woman in his life to enjoy the privilege of being able to insult him for an hour, while a purportedly professional relationship expert - who David happened to know was single because he had researched the woman after their first session together – sat nodding in agreement and telling David, "It's not your turn to *talk*. It's your turn to *listen*", each and every time he tried to speak.

Eventually he could take no more and interjected. "Can I just say something?"
"David, it's not your turn to – "

David cut the insufferable marriage therapist off and turned to face his wife Angelica directly. He decided that he wanted to speak openly from the heart for once. "Look, I realise you've been unhappy for a while, and you should know that this situation isn't exactly fun for me either. I know that I've not been perfect and I am genuinely sorry for that. But you have to understand that all I have tried to be is a good person and a good husband. We've been together for over a decade now, and we've had some good times along the way. I know that there is genuine love between us, even if we don't always show it. There *has* to be! So, before we throw away ten years of marriage, please just stop and ask yourself – isn't our love and happiness worth fighting for? Can't we stop torturing each other and just work *together* for once?"

Angelica fell into a rare silence as she mentally absorbed her estranged husband's plea for love and unity. She stared deep into David's hopeful eyes in astonishment. This was the most David had bared his soul in weeks. Eventually, she turned back to face the therapist.

"And that's another thing. That *voice* of his! Urgh!"

David's shoulders sagged as the therapist nodded in agreement and told him, "Yes, I think Angelica makes a good point. She needs to feel that she is being *listened* to, David! This is not your turn to *talk*, this is your turn to *listen*".

....

Now that she was back in London after her brief stint of posing and exposing herself in the Costa del Sol, former reality TV star Lottie Klünt decided to complete the charade by treating herself to some soft highlights that she hoped would give her hair a natural looking sun-kissed glow. She had heard a lot about a recently opened hair and beauty salon in Soho called *A Cut Above* that was supposedly very trendy, and was happily surprised that they had an appointment slot free for that very afternoon.

"Hi, I'm here! I've got a hair appointment! Sorry I'm late", Lottie wheezed as she came bursting through the doors fifteen minutes after her designated appointment time. "You can't find parking anywhere near here!"

A young assistant, who demonstrated her best multitasking skills as she managed to smile politely, look Lottie straight in the eye and still continue typing a text message to her boyfriend on the phone that appeared to be permanently secured to her hand, greeted Lottie with an excitable squeaky drawl. "No worries darlin', we're running a bit behind on all the appointments today anyway. Hey, aren't you Lottie Klünt?"

"Yes, yes I am. Thank you", Lottie responded proudly. "I knew I recognised you!" the young woman beamed as Lottie beamed back at her. She then took a subtle glance down at Lottie's figure and added, slightly less enthusiastically, "Well I'm good at recognising *faces*, anyway".

The woman grinned proudly at having recognised a household name, while Lottie grinned even more proudly at being the household name that somebody had recognised, and the two women continued to grin wordlessly at one another for far longer than was actually necessary.

Eventually, the young woman broke the dazzlingly toothy silence. "Weren't you in that reality TV show a couple of years back? You all had to live in one house with all the cameras everywhere, and perform tasks for food or something until you were voted out? My boyfriend used to say that you were all acting like trained seals, whatever that means. He liked the weekly wet t-shirt segment, though".

"Yes, I was", Lottie chirped happily, choosing to ignore the comment about the trained seals. "I was also in the show *Celebrity Builders*, where me and nine other celebs competed to see who could learn how to mix the best cement in our underwear, *Celebrity Fashion School* where we had to qualify for a Bachelor of Art Degree in Fashion Design in less than twenty-four hours, and *Celebrity Doctor For A Week – What's That Sound?* where we were challenged to diagnose and guess the cure for the public's various noise-related ailments. Did you see those shows, too?"

The salon assistant's wide smile remained fixed and she ceased blinking for a moment. "Erm, no. I just saw the one where you lived in the house. Did you really get a degree in less than twenty-four hours?"
"Well, not a *real* one, obviously", Lottie admitted, with just a faint trace of embarrassment.
There was another pause.
"Well, anyway", the assistant twittered brightly as she opened up the appointment book, "What name is it, please?"
Lottie waited expectantly for a witty punch line. It didn't come. She then waited for the penny to drop. It didn't, either. Eventually she gave up.
"Lottie Klünt".

"Ah, right. I just thought you might be using some kind of alias, you know, like a proper famous person. Ah, yes. Here you are! Why don't you take a seat in the waiting area while I'll fetch you a cappuccino?"

Lottie sat in the plush waiting area and breezily skimmed through several tabloid magazines that were left out for the customers, privately hoping to catch a glimpse of herself in at least one of them.

Disappointingly, there was nothing about her in *Tomorrow First*, no mention of her in *Better Lives Than Yours* magazine and no reference to her at all in *FASH MAG, GLAD RAGS 'n' W.A.G.S Weekly*.

There wasn't even a token nasty rumour about her in the cheesy *Hi Klass!* bi-weekly publication, despite her agent's repeated attempts to request one on her behalf.

She had just picked up a copy of *Celebs Today* when the salon's assistant came back with her cappuccino and excitedly announced, "Did you happen to see our salon in there? See for yourself, on page fourteen! You're not the only famous person we've had visit us this week".

Lottie thanked the woman and turned to page fourteen. There was nothing. With an inward groan at the cute-but-stupid salon assistant, she then turned to the weekly 'Classy Lassies' section on page *forty* and saw two full pages of photos of Stefani Summerstone, another reality TV star who Lottie had met a few times on the talk show circuit over the years, getting her hair styled at *A Cut Above* and pouting vainly into the mirror.

It didn't take long for Lottie to figure out that Stefani and the salon had arranged a cheesy staged photo opportunity between them to advertise the hair salon, so that they could benefit from the free publicity and that Stefani could take advantage of another business willing to offer her a freebie. There was little subtlety to it, with several references to the beauty salon in the short article and one fairly obvious shot of Stefani leaving the salon with the entire shop frontage in the frame. They had even managed to squeeze in a shot of the salon's curiously ill-thought-out slogan – "*It Grows Back!*" – and as Lottie read the lame article, a couple of thoughts occurred to her.

The first thought that occurred to her as she looked at more than a dozen photographs of Stefani in the salon chair, pouting into her own reflection in the mirror while taking a 'selfie' of herself pouting into her own reflection in the mirror – clearly fully aware that there was a photographer just a couple of metres away taking pictures of her taking photos of herself as she stared at her reflection in the mirror – was that Stefani Summerstone must have all the intelligence, wit and imagination of a small caged budgie.

The second thought that occurred to Lottie as she looked at the blatant crass example of another celebrity freebie was the unhappy realisation that nobody had asked *her* to be photographed getting her hair done!

After paying full price for her hair colouring despite dropping several heavy hints about being famous, Lottie and her new sun-kissed tresses left the salon a couple of hours later, and as she walked the streets trying in vain to remember where on earth she had parked her car this time, she phoned her agent, Teddy.

"Hey, Lottie! Just the person I wanted to talk to!" the agent boomed when the call was transferred to his office. Lottie rolled her eyes. He *always* answered the phone like that! She was just pleased that he had at least said the right name for once.
"Listen, Lottie. I've had a look at tomorrow's tabloids already. You're in quite a few of them, actually. That's some good exposure! My word, you've gotten really fat, haven't you?"

She bit her lip and rolled her eyes again.

"Don't look at me like that", he roared with a knowing laugh, somehow able to accurately recognise Lottie's petulant eye roll even over the telephone. "It's all working in your favour, and so am I! I suggest you put down whatever you're currently eating and get yourself down to the beauty salon for the full works. You're gonna be on live TV tomorrow! Oh, and before I forget… Do you remember a woman called Stefani Summerstone?"

....

41

David glared at the wall clock in angry silence and waited for the marriage therapy session to come to an end. Angelica was still tearing apart every aspect of David's personality and character, while the outrageously unbiased therapist continued to enable and encourage what she referred to as Angelica's "free expression of feelings".

'*That's it*', he concluded to himself, '*I promised myself that I would at least give my marriage one last chance before giving up, and now I have*'.

He felt justifiably annoyed at the unfairness of his wife's attitude and behaviour towards him, but now he was finally beginning to wonder just what he had been fighting so hard for and why he had even been so reluctant to give up on his unhappy marriage in the first place. Angelica was spoiled. She was rude. She spent all of his money, treated him like dirt and worst of all she actually seemed to resent him for being spineless enough to allow her to spend all of his money and treat him like dirt in the first place!

It wasn't as though he was going to be losing a loving and supportive wife, he quite accurately concluded. He had quietly and secretly resented the woman for some time now, but she had quite openly resented him for years. There wasn't even any small compensation of having a partner who was at least good homemaker to console himself with. David often made the unspoken observation that the closest Angelica ever came to hands-on housekeeping was when she pointed one of her manicured talons at parts of their home that the hired cleaners had missed, and even if she ever would have cooked a meal for David, the cold-hearted bitch would have probably made the onions themselves cry!

Brimming with new confidence and an almost alien feeling that felt not unlike self-respect, David realised that he would still have to pay for the pointless therapy session regardless of what happened, and it finally occurred to him that he didn't need to bother waiting until the end. Things were about to change! He could be in control for once!

He fully embraced his newfound backbone as he stood up melodramatically and announced, "That's it! Stop the session! I've had enough! I want a *divorce!*"

The dramatic effect was marginally ruined when the therapist slowly and deliberately turned to glance at the clock, and David clearly saw that there were less than five minutes of the hour-long session left anyway, but he stuck to his guns and tried to maintain his new ballsy look of defiance.

"Thank *fuck* for that!" Angelica exclaimed, as she stood up and put her long designer trench coat on in one sweeping movement, "I thought you'd never say it! I'll let you know who my lawyer is by tomorrow morning. Bye!"

Chapter Four

"Mrs O was absolutely staggering this week on Women's Natter", the nervous personal assistant obediently read aloud from the TV critic section of the previous day's newspaper, *"...by which I mean, of course, that she appears to have been hitting the gin again"*.

He winced and braced himself for the inevitable rant from his notoriously diva-like superior. His boss, Mrs O, had already been in a foul mood all week after receiving an entirely unwelcome offer to be the celebrity face of a company that specialised in feminine incontinence pads for the elderly, and a few well-placed calls had added insult to injury - and caused her enormous ego to suffer a further crushing blow - when she had learned an unhappy truth about the insulting offer; that she had actually only been the company's *seventh* choice of celebrity spokesperson after all. Somehow, that felt so much more offensive. Mercifully, her assistant was spared the onslaught of Mrs O's famously vicious wrath when he was interrupted by a knock on the dressing room door from the show's assistant director.

"Mrs O? Have you got a minute? I would like to go over today's segment with you just once more before we go on the air".

Mrs O waved the man into her dressing room and dismissed her nervous young assistant. "That will be all for now, young... um, *boy*. Go and see how the guests are getting on or something".

The grateful assistant scuttled out of the room as quickly as he could, subtly picking up and taking the daily newspapers with him. The TV critics were very rarely complimentary about the ageing TV personality Mrs O, and it was always a bad day at the office whenever she had been mentioned by one of them. Her recent on-air gaffes had been wildly mocked and she did not take criticism well, as the poor sods that had to read her the reviews had invariably found to their cost. He was finally beginning to suspect that this was partly why her assistants never lasted long enough for her to learn their actual names, although the part about the gin had been fairly accurate and this certainly didn't help matters either.

Pete Waters had been the assistant director on *Women's Natter*, a topical mid-morning TV chat show focussing vaguely on women's issues and celebrity interviews, for only a few weeks. These types of shows had become very popular in the past few years as daytime television schedulers had tried to embrace their target market of housewives, stay-at-home mothers and retired women who represented a large portion of daytime TV's mid-morning/early-afternoon viewership. *Women's Natter* was broadcast just before the station's flagship afternoon show - the unfortunately-named *PM-TV* - and this strategic scheduling back-to-back was often rather crudely referred to in the male-dominated industry as the Bored Housewives' Slot. The short time that Pete had spent working on *Women's Natter* had already proved to be more than enough for him to realise that one of the show's main hosts generally needed a little *extra* attention before the live broadcast.

"Okay, Mrs O. I know we all had our pre-production meeting earlier, but I just wanted to go over today's schedule again with you to make sure we're all nice and clear. You are going to introduce the live segment with today's guests, Stefani Summerstone and Lottie Klünt, two reality TV stars who are both on the show to discuss the issue of *body shaming*. We've just found out that Stefani has actually announced her pregnancy this morning, so we're going to cut this segment short and focus on Stefani a bit more. I've got all your questions written here for you to read through, and we've got you the much bigger autocue font that you've been asking for, so everything should go nice and smoothly".

Tracey Omen-Jones was the famous ex-wife of a bizarre 1970's rock star, who had become a daytime TV presenter and now firmly insisted on being referred to as *Mrs O*, in the misguided belief that this shortened moniker made her sound warmer, friendlier and more approachable. She was none of these things. Not even close. For this reason, nobody had ever dared to tell her that test audiences thought her new alias made her sound weird, or point out the unfortunate coincidence that it was the same name as a popular brand of rubberised marital aids.

Mrs O looked at the list of questions uncertainly. She knew that she had been making a lot of blunders on TV recently, and normally this wouldn't bother her at all as she enjoyed nothing more in life than being noticed, but lately she had been getting the sense that her act was wearing a little thin and she was afraid that she had little else to offer the world. She had long lived up to her eccentric reputation and had always thoroughly enjoyed being thought of as being an unpredictable, flamboyant kind of character, which was an attention-grabbing trick she had learned years before from her first husband, who famously used to refer to himself as "the new Jesus" and claimed to regularly bathe in rats' blood.

Playing up to this character had successfully earned her enough notoriety throughout the decades to keep her name in the public conscious, and had eventually led to her daytime presenting gig on *Women's Natter*, initially more because of the comedic potential she brought than because of her actual popularity. But now that she was firmly on the other side of what could be thought of as 'middle aged' and test audiences weren't responding so well to her anymore, she had tried to reinvent herself as a savvy professional who could discuss serious topical feminine issues without any silly gimmicks or outrageous play acting. Unfortunately, she was beginning to learn that acting serious was actually harder than it looked, and the suspicion was mounting that in reality, her 'crazy act' may not have been such an act all along.

Satisfied that he had at least made an effort to help the blundering daytime host prepare for the live segment, Pete left Mrs O's enormous dressing room and went to go introduce himself to the guests and inform them of the revisions. He knew with weary certainty that Mrs O had been mentally wrapped up in a million other self-involved matters that were far more important to her than a silly little thing like Pete's schedule, but he frankly didn't care. She could embarrass herself on television as much as she pleased as far as Pete was concerned. It didn't matter at all if the critics were ripping her to pieces and the audiences thought she was an idiot – the crucial thing was that people were still watching her.

Whether they loved her, mocked her or loved to hate her was largely irrelevant, and the occasional presenting blunder was potential TV gold where ratings were concerned. The advertisers who funded the show cared about only *numbers* and *language*; large audience shares without any on-air profanities or controversies brought the money in and kept everybody happy. "Which is ridiculous, really", Pete volunteered, as a backstage chat about Mrs O naturally turned into a discussion about media censorship in general. "Once you start over-regulating TV shows, movies, books and so on, you end up censoring real life. You can never tell the same story when you're telling it through the delicate censorship filter of someone else's comfort zone. You just can't". Then again, he mentally concluded, shows like *Women's Natter* were the very architype of watered-down, over-sensitive mindless fodder. Who cared about the actual content? Certainly nobody who worked on mid-morning television, at least as far as Pete could tell.

As Pete neared the large open makeup room where the day's guests were getting ready for the live segment, he heard a series of the most agonising, ungodly screeches echo throughout the studio that chilled him to the bone. He had long ago learned to recognise this particular familiar, blood-curdling sound and abruptly turned around to scurry away in the other direction. He was nearly overtaken by Teddy, Lottie's agent, who was equally keen to be as far away from the makeup room for the exact same reason.

"No bloody way is this a bloody size bloody fourteeeeeeeeeeen!" Lottie shrieked as two costume designers tried with all their might to fasten her into another corset.

"It's like trying to harness the tide!" one of them grunted unhappily as he tried to fasten the uncooperative support garment.

"It'd be easier to squeeze toothpaste back into the tube than to get her into this thing", the other wheezed with irritation as he put his foot on the back of Lottie's chair for support, gripped the two sides of the open corset and thrust himself backwards.

"I can actually *hear* you, y'know!" Lottie angrily snapped at the undiplomatic stylist team, just as the first clasp on the corset succumbed to the pressure and ferociously snapped open once again.

The luckless costume designers had been instructed to make Lottie look as slim as possible today; she was on the show to discuss how she had been unfairly 'body shamed' and how terrible it was in this day and age that people had labelled a perfectly normal, curvaceous woman like herself as 'fat'. As part of the live segment, they were also going to show recent paparazzi photographs that perpetrated to show Lottie minding her own business with a private afternoon on the beach, apparently completely unaware that some mean old photographer had been trying to take unflattering pictures of her. To highlight the unfairness of it all and how misleading these ghastly tabloid photos can be, the

costume designers and makeup artists had been instructed that Lottie had to look as slim and glamorous as possible today.
It was not going as well as they had hoped.

"Alright, try the next size up", Lottie reluctantly gasped, finally admitting defeat as the costume designers exchanged obvious glances of relief. She was already wearing two uncomfortable pairs of Spanx and had her breasts hoisted up so high in a crushing support bra that she was afraid she might topple over if she stood up too quickly, and in spite of all this effort, she still looked sadly at her own reflection as though she was looking at the distorted figure in an old Fun House mirror.
The more they worked on her appearance, the more Lottie felt like a big lumbering sack of unattractiveness.

"This dress doesn't make me look too *thin*, does it?" Stefani Summerstone piped up cheerfully from the next chair, happily aware that it did.
"No, not at all, sweetheart! You look gorgeous, as always" her manager sycophantically gushed, while everybody else in the room except for Lottie smiled and nodded emphatically in agreement.

Stefani Summerstone was also on the show to discuss the issue of 'body shaming', but Stefani's point of view was that people were always accusing her of being *too thin*. This was, naturally, a problem that she and her publicist had entirely fabricated, but somehow it had gained enough momentum to warrant a discussion on daytime television, and she and Lottie had been booked to appear on *Women's Natter* to discuss the same issue but from different perspectives.

Stefani was another reality TV star turned famous-for-being-famous girl who was naturally skinny by any normal standards, despite having given birth to three children during her years in the spotlight, and she had gone to a lot of pains to make herself look even thinner until people had finally started to notice and comment on it, which was her sole reason for doing so.

She used heavy makeup to contour her facial features until she was practically skeletal, perpetually sucked in her cheeks and stomach whenever she was being photographed in some overly revealing outfit that was always deliberately one size too big, and drastically airbrushed photos of herself to waif-like proportions so that she could share them with hundreds of thousands of people online via social media, and then later ask with feigned innocence why on earth people were always judging her weight.

It had always irritated Lottie to her very core, and her irritation was only heightened by the bothersome knowledge that Lottie herself didn't have much of a moral leg to stand on, being no stranger to such cheap tactics. There was just something about the way Stefani actively *enjoyed* being judged that had always annoyed Lottie.

And that wasn't the only thing about Stefani that Lottie found grating…

"I think my dipper is catching my hair when I dand up in dis dress", Stefani loudly informed one of the costume designers, standing up dramatically.
"What?"
"I *daid*, my dipper is catching my hair when I dand up!"
"I'm sorry – your *what* is doing *what*?"
"She said that her *zipper* is catching her hair when she *stands* up. Maybe she needs to change the dress", said Stefani's manager, translating his client's incomprehensible message to the baffled designer.

Stefani had amused the general public and earned their unyielding sympathy with a curious speech impediment that apparently inhibited her from pronouncing an *"st"* sound, although it occasionally varied and was wildly inconsistent. TV audiences seemed to find it completely charming and endearing, and her little speech quirk had quickly earned Stefani a secure place in the nation's heart as soon as she had first stammered her way onto national television in a reality singing competition a few years back.

It made Lottie want to throw up. It wasn't as though she could even sing to begin with. Stefani approached melodies the way a butcher might approach a slaughtered pig carcass, at least as far as Lottie could judge. For someone who was naturally so vocal in her day to day life, as a wannabe singer, Stefani was actually the karaoke equivalent of a kamikaze pilot.

It also hadn't escaped her attention that Stefani would occasionally forget about her own supposedly involuntary speech impairment. It had always baffled her as to why people found it so charming in the first place and somehow managed to ignore the staggeringly obvious fact that she was putting it on. Somehow Stefani seemed to keep getting away with this forced affliction, and audiences had been lapping it up for years.

"We're live in a couple of minutes, ladies!" Pete announced, finally judging it safe to enter the chaotic makeup and dressing area. "Just follow me to the set. Mrs O is going to present your segment just like we rehearsed".
As they walked to the set, it occurred to him that he hadn't had a chance to tell the guests about the slight change to the planned interview, which was Stefani's pregnancy announcement. He unwisely decided that it didn't really matter.

By the end of the broadcast, he would come to regret this decision, although he had no way of knowing this yet. These valuable insights so often come with brutal retrospection, usually only when it was far too late to do anything useful about it anyway.

"I hope I didn't upset you on *TwitchFace* last night", Stefani discreetly muttered to Lottie as they sat on the studio sofas and waited for the cue that they were live on air. "It's all part of the game, ain't it? At least we can laugh it off and show everyone that we're actually friends with this interview".

Lottie smiled and said she didn't mind at all. On the advice of their agents, Lottie and Stefani had engaged in a social media war of words the night before – insulting each other with childish barbs in the hope of creating a bit of publicity and hype for their joint TV interview today. They had been encouraged to taunt one another equally with online gibes that everybody could see, safe in the knowledge that they could both laugh off their 'rivalry' with a friendly daytime TV interview, without any damage to their respective reputations.
The online barbs had been immature and bordering on plain nasty, but they had been enough to entertain their own social media followers and had been shared many times.

"I got loads of new followers by the end of it", Stefani chirped. "Did you?"

Lottie had only seen a minor gain and she strongly suspected that Stefani already knew this. Still, their petty little back-and-forth had at least hyped their TV appearance, as people were left wondering if they were witnessing a genuine celebrity feud or some good-natured banter between two friends, so it certainly hadn't cost anything, and these little online spats were occasionally reported by the tabloids, which meant that there was no such thing as bad exposure as far as Lottie or her agent was concerned.

Some of the more popular messages had been Lottie responding to the self-proclaimed 'people pleaser' Stefani that *'there's more to being a "people pleaser" than just faking orgasms!'*, making light of the fact that the renowned serial-monogamist Stefani had enjoyed multiple romances with minor celebrities, all of which had been shamelessly and theatrically played out in the press.

Stefani in turn had mocked Lottie's lack of romance, spitefully responding, *'I saw @Lottie_Klünt's beach pics in the mags this week. Enjoy the column inches darling, they're the only "inches" you get nowadays!'*, to which Lottie had responded, *'Saying that you once dated @Stefani_Summerstone is like saying that you once saw a fish. It's <u>really</u> not that uncommon!'*

Eventually, the studio fell into a professional silence. They were about to go on the air.

57

"Okay ladies… we are broadcasting live in three, two, one…"

The audience applauded.

"Good morning, Britain! I'm your host, Mrs O, and for those of you who are just tuning in, today we are discussing the issue of *body shaming* here on Women's Natter. Joining us in the studio this morning are reality TV stars Stefani Summerstone and Lottie Klump, both of whom are no stranger to receiving harsh criticisms of their natural body shapes in the press. Ladies, welcome".

"*Danks*, Mrs O!" Stefani squeaked brightly, "I'm really happy to be here today! I think body shaming is an issue that affects all naturally thin girls like me!"

"You and me both!" Mrs O agreed, which was both shameless and untruthful. "But let's look at things from the other side for a moment. Lottie Klunge, how does it make you feel when people point out that you're fat?"

An unnecessarily large and painfully unflattering image of Lottie's recent trip to the beach was projected onto the screen behind them. A second unforgiving image, zooming in on Lottie's bare backside, appeared next to it. She hadn't been warned about this part and suddenly felt like a whale.

"Well, Mrs O. Firstly, thank you and I'm really happy to be on the show too - it's Lottie *Klünt* by the way – but I always think it's important not to use words like 'fat', as that, to me, *is* body shaming. When it comes to body image, how we judge ourselves and how we judge others, I really think…"

"Yeah, I know *exactly* what she means!" Stefani loudly piped up, completely interrupting Lottie, "I always feel like I'm a bit of a fatty when I'm pregnant too, but then people *still* tell me that I'm so thin!"

"Yes, of course!" Mrs O boomed. "For those who don't already know, Stefani Summerstone has announced her pregnancy this morning! Congratulations, Stefani!"

The studio audience suddenly erupted into a huge round of applause as the cameras focussed on Stefani, and Lottie was completely forgotten about. She couldn't believe it! She had gone offline late last night after her online exchange with Stefani and hadn't seen or heard anything about the pregnancy. Stefani had timed it deliberately, Lottie quite accurately concluded, to steal focus from her and set the stage for some rather insulting comparisons. Lottie now had to endure the indignity of being labelled the 'fat' one of the two even when compared to a pregnant woman, and there was no doubt in Lottie's mind that Stefani – in spite of her obnoxiously fake bimbo persona – was well aware of this fact! The applause continued; Stefani stood up and shamelessly flaunted her ridiculously tiny pregnancy bump, and Lottie could do nothing but quietly seethe while only just maintaining a forced smile through gritted teeth.

The presenter began to coo over Stefani as though she was the first woman in human history to ever successfully procreate, and Lottie inadvertently let an involuntary eye roll slip through her mask of composure. She hoped nobody would notice. It wasn't as though this was even Stefani's first pregnancy. She already had three children – to three different fathers – and had already milked the publicity that each relationship and subsequent pregnancy brought her for all it was worth. Her three daughters were called Goldie May, Lambrini Bee and Chardonnay Z, which Stefani bafflingly mispronounced as "Chardon-nee Zee", and now there was a fourth on the way. Lottie couldn't imagine how anyone as stupid, vapid and self-involved as Stefani could ever run a stable household. She barely seemed capable of figuring out how to run a tap!

"*I think* it's important", Lottie interjected, raising her voice in a futile effort to finally put her well-rehearsed point about self-esteem across, "...for young impressionable women who might be concerned by all the body shaming they see in the media, to understand that…"

"Well, as a mother to three young girls, *I* dink…" Stefani

interrupted again, even more loudly.

"Oh, just *stop* it!!" Lottie shouted at Stefani, finally losing her temper and shocking millions of TV viewers, "Shut up for once! Stop acting like being thin and stupid and having lots of babies is some kind of special talent! Shall I put it more clearly for you? *I daid dop it, Defanny, you dupid dick!!!*"

The studio audience fell into a stunned silence, as did Mrs O and Stefani, although Stefani didn't completely forget about the cameras and theatrically portrayed a wide-eyed gasp like an adorable hurt puppy; all the while strategically clutching her stomach as though Lottie's words were going to physically hurt her somehow.

"Well... this is the kind of lively debate that occurs when we tackle these hard-hitting topics here on Women's Natter", Mrs O rallied, for once finally demonstrating a rare moment of calm professionalism in the face of her guest's unexpected rant. "I think this seems like a good time for a commercial break. We'll be right back after these messages, so let's say a warm thanks to our guests today – Stefani Summerstone and Lottie *Kunt*".

As one, Lottie, her agent backstage and director Pete Waters simultaneously screamed inwardly in horror.

Chapter Five

"How's the salad?"
"Smells good. How's your fish steak?"
"Looks lovely".

Scandal-ridden ex-footballer Roger Scott looked at his wife. There was something he couldn't quite put his finger on. He was slowly beginning to sense that maybe she wasn't altogether happy about something, although he couldn't possibly imagine what that could be, what he could do about it or - his attention was momentarily distracted by an incredibly glamorous woman in a low cut, barely there dress who had just entered the restaurant. What was he thinking about just now?

"Would you like another water?" Cherlene asked, purely for the sake of having something to say.
"No thanks. I'm still full from my last one", Roger politely responded with just a faint trace of weary disappointment in his voice. Cherlene didn't allow him to have alcohol in public anymore, not since the drink-driving scandal. Image was everything, at least to his wife. How he longed for a beer.

What *was* he thinking about just a moment ago? A brief flash of eye contact from the waiter made Roger – for no obvious logical reason - think about his own hair

suddenly, which he then checked in the reflection of his spoon for some time. ´*Still perfect*´, he reassured himself after a few minutes with some satisfaction. ´*Not a hair out of place*´.
Was he thinking something about his hairstyle, perhaps?

"It's a pity I've already eaten today", Cherlene lamented conversationally.
Roger gave a vague shrug of half acknowledgement. He was preoccupied with his thought, or at least preoccupied trying to remember what his thought had been. He had the feeling that he had been on the cusp of thinking or realising something that might have been somewhat important. Possibly.

"Excuse me, Sir", a waiter very politely interjected, tapping Roger lightly on the shoulder, "I think something has just fallen out of your pocket".

"Oh, thanks", Roger smiled, taking the object in his hand. "It's part of my new security system at home. We have these electronic keys now. Much more secure.
Sometimes I do still lose the key fobs though, but I just have to type 5978 into the security keypad at the front door and I can still get in. Same as my PIN number. You can't be too careful with security these days. Especially when you're famous".

Cherlene gave another very deliberate, very heavy and very meaningful sigh. Even the people on the opposite tables noticed this time.

Oh, right – Roger's brain finally nudged his train of thought back on track - he was thinking about his wife! There seemed to be something *off* about her lately. Something different. Something he couldn't quite put his finger on.

"The food *looks* great though", Cherlene added sadly, "It's just a pity I don't have anyone to talk to".

"Hmm?" Roger responded, turning back from the attractive looking waitress that had just caught his attention. He apparently didn't happen to notice the scolding look of warning from his wife though, whose patience was running out far more quickly than he was even close to realising.

He shrugged noncommittally and realised that his train of thought had become derailed once again. What *was* he thinking about just now?

....

"What *were* you thinking just now?" Teddy shouted at Lottie, who had that morning very swiftly and suddenly become his number one most problematic client. They

65

were backstage in the dressing area of the *Women's Natter* studio and trying to mentally absorb the disastrous TV appearance Lottie had just made moments earlier. As a talent agent to the terminally talentless, he would normally encourage his clients to do absolutely anything they could to earn themselves even a morsel of precious exposure, since his clients rarely did anything worthwhile, nor did they have actual deserving careers to fall back on. Public exposure was the lifeblood of the talentless, providing the oxygen of publicity that would keep them under the precious spotlight for as long as their fifteen minutes would allow. Practically anything would do and few things were off limits since there were no apparent limits as to how exposed a person might become, but he also knew how the general public loved few things more than a public enemy that they could all turn on, and that Lottie had suddenly made herself such a target in just a few seconds of live TV that she might as well be wearing a bullseye. He knew that her little outburst on national television this morning would not be popular in the least, and guiltily realised that it would take a far more talented agent than himself to drag Lottie out of the negative PR pit she had blundered into, which is exactly why he resorted to the all-purpose contingency plan that all agents employ in times like these, and simply blamed the client.

"We *discussed* this! You were supposed to be on TV to show everyone how you were a *victim* of body shaming! That you aren't as fat in real life as the pap pics suggest and that people should have sympathy for you. People *like* victims! People *don't like* bullies, and that's what you've made yourself look like by shouting at a pregnant woman, even if it *was* that gormless thicko *Defanny Dumb-as-a-stone!*"

A few people nervously glanced around to see if Stefani Summerstone had been within earshot of Teddy's rather unkind, uncensored but not-entirely-undeserving observation. Thankfully, she was still on the set enthusiastically posing for photos with audience members, regardless of whether they actually asked her for one. It suddenly occurred to Pete - the assistant director whose chief director had gone home during the commercial break with a conveniently timed migraine - that there were a lot more crew members backstage all of a sudden to witness Lottie's scolding than there normally were. They were probably more interested in what was going to be said about Mrs O, he quite accurately surmised. Or simply trying to avoid her!

"Urgh, when is she ever *not* pregnant? We all know that she made her announcement *today* of all days just to upstage me. Besides, it wasn't *all* my fault", Lottie protested passionately. She felt angry, humiliated and frustrated at her farce of a TV appearance, and so like any true celebrity she resorted to her an all-purpose contingency plan of her own, which was to simply blame anybody and everybody else.
She fervently continued, "What about Mrs O? Mrs 'Oh-

What-Was-*She*-Thinking', more like! Did you hear what she called me? Live on national TV, she called me Lottie *Ku* - I don't even want to repeat it! But you all heard it, didn't you? You all heard it, and so did half of Britain!"

This was true. The one saving grace to the catastrophic morning, as far as Lottie's agent could see, was that people were probably going to be far more interested in Mrs O's inadvertent slip of the tongue than Lottie's outburst. Mrs O had uttered the one word that TV audiences found unforgivable, as did the regulatory bodies that monitor and censor broadcast television. It was clear to anyone that Mrs O had now firmly cemented her reputation as a laughing stock, and her accidental on-air profanity live on mid-morning television was guaranteed to earn complaints, reprisals and possibly a large fine for the network. Teddy tried to console himself with the assurance that Lottie's little rant at Stefani would be overshadowed by Mrs O's unfortunate lapse in concentration. Lottie could dodge the bullet on this one, he told himself. Nobody would remember her outburst compared to Mrs O's blunder, he decided.

'*Or Mrs O has just guaranteed that the worst TV appearance Lottie Klünt has ever made is about to go viral and be remembered forever*', the traitorous thought uttered in his mind, despite his best efforts to ignore it.

"Besides", Lottie continued, determined to fully explore absolutely any point of view that would render herself blameless over the PR disaster of the morning's events, "I thought that being noticed was supposed to be a *good* thing. I thought that you wanted us to act like we had some kind of rivalry or celeb feud. You said that it would give us publicity, and that was all that mattered! You were the one who told us to insult each other on *TwitchFace*. Surely me shouting at a pregnant woman on TV isn't *that* much different from me insulting a non-pregnant woman online?"

Teddy didn't answer. He was momentarily stumped. There was a clear and defined difference, he knew, between an online social media spat to generate a bit of publicity - which was obviously a good thing - and an actual real life example of a real insult that had genuine feeling behind it - which was obviously a bad thing - although when put on the spot in that moment he wasn't precisely clear or defined on what the clear and defined difference was.

"What exactly is *TwitchFace*?" Pete asked, suddenly feeling like a dinosaur.

69

"It's the newest thing in social media. Every celeb has a *TwitchFace* profile!" Teddy happily explained to the room at large. He felt like he was on familiar territory here at least. "It's really simple and easy. You create your profile and then, well, what you do is write what's called a *Twitch* status, which is just words, or post what's called a *Twitch-Face* status if it's uploaded with a 'selfie' picture. You then ask the people who follow you - yeah, people *follow* your profile on *TwitchFace* - whether they want to *Love It* or *Shove It*. So, you always try to get more *Loves* than *Shoves*, because that means that you're popular. Your followers in turn can opt to *Share-Face* your *Twitch*, which means that they share it with their own *TwitchFace* followers, who may also choose to *Follow-Through* and then they become your followers too. You can also *Insta-Twitch* with someone personally if you want to chat with them, or you can assign them as your personal *Instant-Twits* if you want to exchange instant direct personal messages or nudey pictures that none of your *TwitchFace* followers can see, *Love, Shove, Follow-Through* or *Share-Face*. Understand?"

"Eh?"
"It's like a cross between *Facebook* and *Twitter*."
"Oh, right."

Teddy noticed that the room had suddenly fallen silent. He looked behind him, and saw Stefani strutting backstage and making a direct beeline for Lottie. He held his breath in anticipation, as did the entire backstage crew and especially Lottie.

"Stefani, I'm sorry about..." Lottie began, but was immediately cut off.

"*Danks* for dat! I bet dat's going to get me dousands of new *TwitchFace* followers!" Stefani beamed at Lottie, radiating utter delight in every syllable. There was no hint or sign that she had taken any offence to whatever Lottie had said during their brief interview. Lottie even began to wonder if the woman had actually heard her, although she quite clearly had. Stefani could be infuriatingly single-minded at times, and was apparently incapable of registering or acknowledging any kind of insult, not unless someone was willing to explain it to her several times, it appeared. It was baffling. She seemed as though she was just delighted to be receiving attention whatever the context. Somehow, it didn't make Lottie feel any better though.

"I dink I'll post something about how I need a new car. Maybe someone'll send me one as a promo freebie. You never know!"

Lottie's jaw fell open at the sheer brazen attitude. She wasn't sure whether to pity the girl or admire her. How could anybody be so genuinely pleased to have been insulted like that?

"Dere's a couple of paparazzi people outside. Do I look like I've been crying?" Stefani cheerfully continued, as she picked a lemon wedge out of the glass of water that had served as her lunch and dabbed it under her eyes, which made her eyes water and her heavy eye makeup run slightly. The overall effect that this caused did indeed make it look as though she had been crying.

"Danks, again! Let me know if you want another *TwitchFace* argument sometime. *Dat* was *fun!*" she twittered, brightly. And with that, she sauntered away.

The following day, the second biggest selling national tabloid was one that published photos of Stefani leaving the TV studio with the accompanying headline - *'Pregnant Stefani Sobs After Lottie Klünt's Scathing TV Attack'*

The biggest selling tabloid of the day ran with the headline - *'Mrs O Suspended After On-Air C-Word Disaster'.*

....

Cherlene Scott sat in the restaurant picking miserably at her salad and glared at her ex-footballer husband again. He had the familiar glossy eyed stare that she sadly knew all too well. She referred to it as his 'switched off' mode. It was almost as though there was a little light behind Roger's eyes that seemed to go out the second that conversation strayed into unfamiliar territory, which for Roger meant any subject other than himself or the attractiveness of others, especially women. Society, politics, travel, culture - all of these topics and more were complete no-go areas. Hair products, pretty girls and being Roger Scott were traditionally his favourite subjects of conversation.

For her own amusement, Cherlene sometimes tried to learn and identify which particular glossy eyed expression Roger was demonstrating as he stared blankly into space, and mused upon what the expression meant he might be thinking about. After a few silent moments of unreciprocated gazing, she noticed a subtle flash of satisfaction appear momentarily on his face that would have been virtually impossible for anyone else to detect, and this indicated that he was thinking about something to do with his own appearance. Perhaps he had been contemplating just how good looking he was, and the hint of satisfaction was the moment when he reached the happy conclusion that he was in fact very good looking indeed. Cherlene had spent countless hours over the years yearning for conversation while staring at Roger's blank expression - in restaurants, dinner parties, nightclubs, birthday parties, soirees, social events and at home - and she had long ago learned to recognise all of his subtle tells. A young woman walked past in a skimpy off-the-shoulder dress, and Roger's blank expression suddenly took on a sort of barely masked pining quality, as he tried hard not to notice the woman but couldn't resist stealing a quick glance. Cherlene was used to this too. He looked longingly at other women in the same way that a hungry dog might look longingly at a large steak. This thought took her on a logical left turn, and she looked down at Roger's untouched food that also seemed destined to spend the evening being ignored.

"You're not eating tonight?"
"Hmm? What?"
"I asked if you weren't eating tonight. You haven't touched your fish steak. Aren't you hungry?"
"Hmm? What? No, no I'm not hungry".

Cherlene had already known this even without asking. Roger had filled up earlier on protein shakes and his bi-weekly steroid injections. He just didn't seem to have the concentration required to sit through regular big meals. *'Maybe he eats when he is with the other women´*, she pondered to herself without much feeling, as she wondered what excuse her philandering husband would use to explain his inevitable absence at home later that evening.

She looked down at her own simple salad and picked at it idly. She had spent a small fortune on her own appearance that week, from the various agony-inducing and expensive treatments she had endured from someone who advertised himself as the 'dermatologist to the stars', to the expensive personal trainer she had hired to shout at her and tell her to go running each morning, as well as the extortionate fees she was paying a dietician to essentially tell her not to eat. She was determined to look her absolute best in anticipation of her divorce announcement and big tell-all interview with *Celebs Today*. She had even chosen a beautiful horsetail that her hairdresser was planning to use as hair extensions for the accompanying photo-shoot, as horsehair was 'virgin' hair and apparently could look more natural than anything that a human being could possibly grow. The timing was almost right. She was almost ready and was actually quite excited. She could hardly wait to see all the new opportunities that would come from being a public figure once she announced her plans to divorce her cheating husband; interviews, photo-shoots, advertising, television appearances - Cherlene dreamed of being the nation's most glamorous 'wronged woman', accepted into the public's hearts and becoming a household name.

Roger still had no idea.

She looked across at her husband, who at that moment seemed to be completely enthralled by staring down in deep concentration at his bare forearms and subtly flexing his muscles occasionally. She briefly wondered what it was that made his own arms apparently better company than she was - they were certainly occupying his attention in this moment more than she ever could - and then began to wonder just how much being famous had changed and affected Roger overall. It had often been said that those who are truly famous live in such an isolated world, one so far removed from an average person's reality, that they are never really able to grow up from the age they were when they had first achieved fame. Especially child stars, who often remain confined to a confusing and unsatisfying bubble of mental adolescence for the rest of their lives. The *Age of Stagnation*, this was sometimes referred to as. This little theory might explain why Cherlene often felt as though she was actually married to an excitable horny seventeen-year-old masquerading as a grown man. She wondered whether fame would ultimately have the same effect on her.

So many people sought fame, she had observed, but so few people ever seemed willing to let it go.

Cherlene had been convinced that being married to Roger was different when he had been a successful professional footballer, although now that she was beginning to actually look back and reflect on things retrospectively, she honestly wasn't so sure that it had been. Football had been Roger's passion, his dream and his only talent. Without it, he was aimless and always seemed to be looking for the next cheap thrill to fulfil whatever gap his dead professional career had left him with. Or at least that was the way it had seemed to Cherlene, who was only now beginning to sense that she might have been entirely wrong about this all along. Maybe the truth was that Roger was behaving exactly as he always had done, but the glory of being a famous successful footballer's wife had simply rendered her blind to the flip side of being married to an empty-headed, adulterous pretty boy. Perhaps Cherlene's rose-tinted glasses had simultaneously become lost along with Roger's football career, and without them, she could finally see the red flags that had been there all along for what they really were. Or maybe it simply had something to do with his complete inability and unwillingness to understand the concept of monogamy. Whatever had gone wrong along the way, Cherlene now felt certain that she would have the last laugh at least, which was probably the best thing most people could hope for in matters of the heart.

Noticing a couple of photographers gathering outside to see who might be leaving the notorious celebrity hotspot, Cherlene indicated to Roger that it was now time to leave the restaurant. The actual business of eating a meal together was irrelevant. The sole reason for going to the fashionable restaurant was to be *seen* leaving it.

"Well, that was a lovely meal and another beautiful evening", Cherlene loudly enthused while gazing romantically at her husband, as they walked out of the restaurant to blinding camera flashes. Between them, she and Roger had barely taken five bites of food all evening.

"Hmm?" Roger responded again, somewhat less romantically. He had become momentarily distracted by his handsome reflection in the restaurant window, and was now thinking of a clever fool-proof excuse as to why he wouldn't be home later tonight.

'Cherlene will never, ever suspect a thing', he thought to himself proudly.

Chapter Six

David sat in his lawyer's office in unhappy silence, shocked at what he had just heard. It was an expensive place for a person to sit in silence, whether it was a happy one or not, and for this reason his lawyer smiled a slow, satisfied smile that indicated he was very happy indeed. Then he remembered himself.

"I just really don't understand how all of this can be possible. Is the horrid beast seeking a divorce from *me* or a divorce from *reality*!? She can't possibly think she can get away with all of this?" David blurted out suddenly, wisely ending an expensive few moments of quiet mental absorption.

"I'm afraid that everything Mrs Paige is doing is well within the confines of the law", came the predictable but nonetheless soul-destroying response. "You might have paid for the car, but it is registered in her name, so she is entitled to keep it. Both of your names are on the deeds of the marital home, regardless of who is actually paying the mortgage, so you cannot technically make her leave and she is entitled to seek residence there. The fact of the matter is that you have agreed to leave the house of your own accord when she asked you to. You had a choice. You could have legally refused".

"You haven't met my ghastly wife yet, have you? Let's

just say that she speaks three languages and has never bothered to understand the word *no* in any of them!" David grumbled, sadly.

"You could cohabit?" the lawyer suggested. "You're legally entitled to. You can't force her to leave the marital home, but *she* can't force *you* to leave, either. Perhaps if you decided that you wanted to cohabit throughout your separation, that would gently encourage her to find accommodations of her own, if she's so determined to live separately. I appreciate that it's not exactly a desirable living scenario, but I'm sure you could handle it as a temporary solution, at least".

"You wouldn't say that if you had ever actually lived with the horrible woman. Frankly, at this point, if humanity were suddenly destroyed and Angelica and I were the last two humans on Earth, I would be trying to repopulate the planet with the dog before I even thought of trying with her", David countered, with genuine feeling.

"Ah, yes. That's something else we need to discuss", the lawyer responded, in a sympathetic yet unmistakably ominous tone that suggested whatever he was about to tell David about was going to be bad news, expensive news or both. "About the dog…"

David fell into a stunned, unhappy silence once more.

....

Cherlene Scott, meanwhile, sat in her own lawyer's office and was feeling – she wasn't exactly sure what she was feeling – but she was brimming with all kinds of new emotions and felt sure that she was doing the right thing. She was excited, slightly apprehensive and positively giddy. She wondered briefly if there was something that was stopping her from feeling sad and whether this was normal. She knew exactly how underhanded it was to make arrangements to leave her husband without even letting him know anything about it until he physically received the divorce papers, but that was all part of her revenge. She wanted him to be shocked by this. She wanted to catch him off guard, so that she could feel as though *she* was the one emerging from the proverbial pile of excrement smelling of roses for once. Besides, most of his behaviour throughout their marriage had happened in secret behind her back anyway. There was almost a poetic irony to it.

'Roger deserves this', she thought quietly.
'This has been a long time coming', she reassured herself.
'This is the start of a whole new chapter in my life', she mused, with varying degrees of confidence.

But the loudest thought of all screamed, *'I'm going to be really, really famous'*, as she envisioned her post-separation magazine interviews with a tantalising buzz of excitement.

"Just sign here", the lawyer told her as he presented her with the final document of the divorce petition.
She signed. There was no going back now.

"Perhaps we ought to do that again", her lawyer wearily advised, with a subtle nod of indication towards the large, childish love heart that Cherlene had punctuated her signature with. "That might be considered a tad inappropriate, in the circumstances".

He printed off another copy. She signed. There was definitely no going back this time.

....

Needless to say, David's separation from Angelica was not going well. More specifically, it was not going well for *one* of them. It had begun as a tough week for David. Then it had been a tougher week. Then it had been a particularly tough month. After that, things had more or less become progressively worse. Angelica had begun divorce proceedings from David with more gusto than he had ever known her to commit to anything, and she had already taken every possible legal advantage she could while David was still metaphorically putting his boots on.

Neither of them had been married before and their marriage had been a decade-long, bumpy road of ups and downs – mostly downs – but Angelica seemed to be taking to divorce like a duck would take to water. She was a natural. To Angelica, the process of divorce was one that should be as swift, brutal and deadly as a mousetrap. Only less pretty. David was taking to divorce like a duck would take to the M25. He simply didn't stand a chance.

"You mentioned before that you thought that your wife might have been unfaithful. Is that an avenue we're still willing to explore?" his lawyer asked happily, presenting the rather hurtful question to his client in what David considered to be an inappropriately jovial tone. There was a trace of optimism in the lawyer's voice that indicated in a less than subtle way that he hoped the answer would be 'yes'. Clearly, being a divorce lawyer inevitably meant forgoing certain subtleties and delicate tact. Probably you could be a sensitive lawyer or you could be a successful lawyer, David considered, but you certainly couldn't be both.

'If only I could talk to my younger self, I'd tell him to forget everything he thinks he knows about life, to give up any notion of hope, and just become a soulless divorce lawyer. At least I'd have a chance at being rich in my wretchedness', he grumpily thought to himself. The train of thought that this prompted took him on a short journey of viewpoints about lawyers, the last one of which reminded David just how expensive his legal representative was and why he shouldn't waste time lamenting his failed marriage and general failed existence. Especially not when he was being billed by the hour. He considered the question again. Had Angelica been unfaithful?

David winced at the word. *Unfaithful.* He was okay with the belittling. He could handle a little dishonesty. He didn't mind a bit of good-natured, soul destroying emotional blackmail, power struggles, scathing insults and downright nasty slanging matches. At least he and Angelica had engaged in those things *together*, as some kind of terrifyingly toxic yet equally matched marital team. There was an almost twisted sense of balance to it, a kind of sadistic melody of symmetry that was more or less fair in its equal distribution of utter misery. Even among the emotionally demented, there still needed to be a *ying* to one's *yang*, or at least that's the way it had always seemed to David. The Paige's marriage had built its foundations on this idea, as though the very bedrock of their relationship was based on a kind of Emotional Paralympics competition that put everyone involved on an even footing. It wasn't perfect by anyone's standards, but at least man knew where he stood in that respect. But unfaithfulness? That crossed a big line as far as David was concerned. It just seemed so underhanded, so deceptive and so humiliating.

"No", he answered, simply.

"Then I'm afraid we really don't have much to go on at this stage. Unless we can convince Mrs Paige to take a more amicable approach".

David sighed again. He needed a break and decided to go for a lunchtime drink or six. He did not want to hear the words 'divorce' or 'separation' again for a very long time. He definitely didn't want to hear the word 'lawyer'. His phone rang. It was Ashton Cain, his only superior at the magazine.

"David, forget about lunch. I want to talk about Cherlene Scott's divorce!"

Chapter Seven

The repetitive wailing from Roger's cheesy ringtone filled the apartment with the ugliest noise pollution as his mobile phone began to ring again. For reasons known only to him, Roger had chosen a club song that sounded like a drug-crazed parrot in a blender to replace the standard ring tone noise that any rational grownup might choose for their handset. Roger had been trying to ignore the obnoxious siren of his phone ringing all afternoon – which by now even *he* was beginning to find grating - but after missing at least half a dozen phone calls within the past fifteen minutes he finally reached the conclusion that someone probably had something quite urgent to tell him. He lurched around the tiny apartment he had secretly rented months before, looking under all the haphazardly discarded clothes and negligee that littered the room until he finally found his phone, which had fallen underneath the lovingly overused bed - along with several pieces of expensive underwear, multiple condoms, a designer watch, two long-forgotten wallets and another lost mobile phone that he had reported as stolen months ago.

He looked at the screen. His P.R. agent, Clive Maxwell, was calling him.

"This is either going to be something good or something bad", Roger said aloud as he contemplated hitting the 'reject call' button. "Although I guess that's probably true of most things", he added, which was about as much depth and philosophy as he was realistically capable of. "Roger! At long last! It's Clive, your *agent*. I've been trying to get hold of you all afternoon!" Clive loudly and irritably began the conversation when Roger finally answered the phone. "Why didn't you *tell* me what Cherlene was planning? Things like this are *important* to an agent, Roger!"

Roger thought about this for a moment. He was confused. What *was* Cherlene planning? He vaguely recalled his wife talking about a book club or something... Or was it a brunch club? Was that a thing that people did? She probably almost certainly did *something* with her time that occasionally required a little planning, even if Roger couldn't remember at that moment exactly what it was. Whatever her little mundane activities were, and however much of a mystery they were to her husband, Roger's dawdling mind finally concluded that they probably wouldn't be of much concern to Clive though.

"I have no idea what you're talking about", he eventually answered, honestly.

"Really? *Really?* You really don't know? Well, I suppose that's probably true of most things, if we're being frank!" Clive responded, adding his own brand of irritable philosophy to the conversation. "In fact, *I Have No Idea What You're Talking About* should be the title of your autobiography, should you ever get around to letting me commission one!"

PR guru Clive Maxwell was generally far more mild mannered than this when communicating with his clients, but news of Cherlene's surprise divorce stunt had caught him uncharacteristically off guard and he was trying not to become flustered by it all. Then again, Roger had never seemed to possess the imagination or processing power to detect an insult if it was mild enough or involved words with more than two syllables, so it was all the same to him.

Clive mentally regained his composure and continued, "Listen to me carefully. I've just received word about a big feature that's going to be published tomorrow morning in *Celebs Today* magazine. She's *divorcing* you, Roger! She's done a big exposé tell-all interview with them that's apparently going to destroy your reputation, and that's probably just the beginning! I'm going to make an educated guess and say that you're not at home right now, but trust me – Cherlene is not going to be there when you return. Did you *really* have no idea about any of this?!"

"None whatsoever", Roger answered, aghast. He gestured towards the door, giving a subtle indication to the escort, who was currently naked in his bed, that their afternoon session had come to an end and that she should leave.

"Okay, well I've already got our lawyers ready to go through her interview with a fine-tooth comb as soon as it's published. But we need to have an emergency meeting to discuss what dirt she might have on you, what skeletons you might have in your closet and what we can do about it. This will likely take some time, as I'm sure even you must realise. It sounds like Cherlene is really out for revenge this time, Roger! This could be the end of you, professionally speaking. She is going to claw her way into the spotlight at the expense of your reputation unless we act *very* quickly! This could really hurt us".

"My baby Cherlene's really divorcing me, though? I just... I can't... I mean, I wasn't even..." Roger stammered, still completely in shock as he tried to comprehend the unexpected development. "This is really terrible news. I always thought our marriage was, well... not bad. I mean, I suppose she *has* been a little quiet lately, now that I think about it. I always felt sure that she was happy with me though, that she loved me and all that stuff. Clive, you have been my agent and my friend for fi... si... sev... well, I don't know how many years. But you've been by my side through thick and thin, and you're the smartest man I know! Tell me honestly; is this *really* the end? Is there *anything* I can do? What can I do to make this all alright?"

Clive Maxwell took a moment to give this important question some meaningful consideration. Roger waited in hopeless expectation. Clive finally had his complete and full attention, which was quite possibly the first and only time that this had ever occurred throughout their entire professional relationship.

Finally, he answered. "I don't know. Maybe reality TV?"

There was a sudden anti-climactic pause. Clive realised that more was expected from him. Partially thinking aloud and partially just hoping to fill the discomfited silence, Clive continued, "Although it would be better to raise your profile a bit more first. We might have to just accept the fact that the public is going to see you as a cad now. Give me a new story to work with - one that doesn't involve Cherlene-bloody-Scott! The press just *love* a 'woman scorned'. They're the bane of my existence!"

Roger slumped heavily onto the bed, stupefied and muted with bewilderment. He could barely process what he had just been told, although even *he* would have to admit that this was probably true of most things…

It should have been a good week for David. He had spent weeks putting in all the legwork for *Celebs Today*'s biggest exclusive of the year – 'Cherlene Scott's Surprise Divorce Announcement' – and when it had finally hit the newsstands, sales had gone through the roof. Professionally speaking, it should have been a very proud moment. Physical sales had exceeded 463,000 for that week in the UK alone, which, rather satisfyingly, was at least 50,000 more than their rivals *Tomorrow First* had managed, and the credit should have largely gone to David. In order to prevent any leaks or rumours that would spoil their celebrity exclusive, David had taken a rare hands-on approach to the whole feature, from being present at the glamorous photo shoot to personally preparing and conducting the interview – he had even personally added a creative spin to many of Cherlene's quotes whenever she had been in danger of giving an answer that could technically be considered libellous or boring. He had also had the brilliant idea of releasing a teaser of her interview on the *Celebs Today* website in the very early hours of the morning before the magazine hit the newsstands, strategically timed so that some of the other tabloids had enough time to report on the fact that Roger Scott was being served with divorce papers, while also leaving them with little chance to actually research or prepare any new content themselves. They were left with no choice but to simply quote the small section *Celebs Today*'s exclusive that was offered online, reluctantly providing free advertising to the hotly anticipated magazine issue.

The carefully crafted interview painted a dramatically pitiful picture of the Scott's marriage, portraying Cherlene as a woefully neglected but loyal wife who had been reluctantly pushed out of her relationship by her self-centred, drink-driving, cheating, has-been, diva of a husband. It was some of David's most creative work to date, a tantalisingly scandalous character assassination so carefully worded that it was legally defensible from every angle.

He could have almost felt quite sorry for Roger, who had apparently still been completely oblivious to the fact that his wife was secretly planning on becoming his ex-wife and destroying his reputation until the last possible moment. Well, David could have felt sorry for him had it been anybody else, but Roger Scott wasn't someone who roused or inspired much sympathy in people, least of all David. Besides, public shaming of her cheating husband had been Cherlene's motivation all along, which was exactly why she had sought to end her marriage and humiliate him in such a public way. It was a bit of a spiteful trick, admittedly, although compared to the viciousness of David's own estranged wife and her gleeful assassination of their marriage and life together, Cherlene was still leaps and bounds more merciful in comparison.

By the standards of tabloid journalism, Roger's public shaming was par for the course and all part of the fame game. David's conscience remained blissfully untroubled.

It *should have* been a good week. Unfortunately, David's boss Ashton Cain had decided to take a rare interest in the proceedings in spite of David's personal handling of the exclusive, and that had rather soured the experience for David. The addition of Ashton Cain's presence to any given situation was like the inclusion of a migraine to an algebra exam. It would be untrue to say that he had a general tendency to dictate or direct magazine features. He adopted a slightly different management style, which was to encourage his staff to work independently and make their own decisions while taking the time to object loudly and furiously to whatever they independently decided upon anyway. It was like taking a driving test on a road with hundreds of speed cameras but no indication of the actual speed limit. Ashton and David had clashed all week and had argued ferociously over almost every little detail of the exclusive, but somehow David had actually managed to stand his ground for the first time in their professional relationship, until Ashton had eventually lost interest and found somebody lower ranking to antagonise.

David had even managed to convince Ashton not to include an acknowledgement of the private eye Cherlene had hired or any of the incriminating photos that actually proved Roger had been committing adultery, by telling him that Cherlene's narrative of being cheated on yet again would be more than enticing enough on its own. There was also the fairly recent legal grey area of *Super Injunctions* that were often a popular Get Out Of

Jail Free card amongst scandal-dodging celebs to consider. Especially in recent years. Publishing the stealthily-taken photos of Roger's lovers that had been acquired by Cherlene's private detective might risk prompting some kind of a legal gagging order that would not only prohibit the media from reporting the details of a story, but also even forbid them to acknowledge the existence of the injunction itself. Since this particular eventuality could potentially scupper the whole exposé, Ashton reluctantly agreed, reasoning that Roger Scott cheating on his wife was nothing new anyway and that the focus should be more on the new woman scorned rather than the old serial adulterer. For now, Cherlene should be the central character in this tale. Besides, they could always come back to the details at a later date and shame Roger retrospectively with another revelation of his extra marital affairs on a quieter week when they had little else to report on. This happened quite a lot in tabloid journalism.

'Cherlene Scott's Surprise Divorce Announcement' had very much been David's personal project throughout every headache-inducing stage until the very end, when the sales figures were confirmed and Ashton shamelessly took all the credit! It was sickeningly unfair, and once again there was absolutely nothing that David could do about it.

Cherlene Scott checked herself in the mirror of the hotel lobby for what seemed like the hundredth time, until she was completely satisfied she didn't have a single hair out of place and that her outfit was perfect. She vainly practiced her trademark pouting face once again – which didn't lose any of its ridiculousness even after unceasing amounts of repetition - put on her enormous sunglasses in spite of the looming thunderclouds outside and then gestured at the hotel porter that he could finally open the door for her. She knew that Roger had been officially served with her divorce petition that very afternoon, but their separation was the furthest thing from her mind at that moment as she strutted outside towards her waiting chauffeur. There was another angry roar of loud thunder and several flashes of lightning in the sky as Cherlene was instantly surrounded by paparazzi photographers, all of whom had braved the stormy weather all afternoon to wait for her, and they were now eagerly shouting questions about Roger at her and submerging her in a dazzling blaze of blinding camera flashes. The noise was deafening. Cherlene pretended to ignore all of this, maintaining a dignified silence while holding her head high and keeping her lips firmly pursed until she reached the open car door, at which point she stopped momentarily and very discreetly placed a small folded piece of paper into the unresisting hand of the nearest paparazzi photographer.

Moments after her chauffeur-driven car had sped away, the baffled photographer opened the handwritten note she had given him. It read:

I've heard that Paris Hilton used to send the paps her weekly schedule in advance so that they always knew where to find and take pics of her, so I guess if I'm going to be famous like Paris then you should always know where to catch me. Here's my work schedule…

Cherlene ~~Scott~~ TBD!

Monday – **Hanging around at the hotel until further notice.**

(p.s. If I decide to go shopping or something, I'll make sure to put it on Twitchface beforehand).

Hugz n kisses!

There was no other information other than a large, crudely drawn love heart at the bottom.

Chapter Eight

"Hello? Who is this?"
"It's Lottie. Sorry I'm a bit late. Parking nightmare, as usual!"
"Right, right. Oh, *Lottie*! Just the person I wanted to talk to! Erm, what do you want?"
"We have an appointment, Teddy! Can you let me inside? Listen to the thunder, it's raining bucket loads out here!"
"Oh! Right, right! Yes, of course".

Teddy put down the intercom phone and buzzed Lottie into the building. His agency office was on the top floor so he knew that he had a few minutes to try and remember why he had arranged an appointment with Lottie while she negotiated the four flights of steep stairs. He felt thankful that Lottie wasn't one of his more athletic clients as he searched through various notebooks and clumsily discarded scraps of paper that littered the room for clues. Teddy had always considered himself a deep thinker who spent half of his time forming ideas that would help his semi-famous clientele negotiate whatever careers they were clinging on to or whatever illusions of grandeur they were trying to project. He was also a deeply disorganised man who spent the other half of his time trying to remember what these ideas were and trying to make sense of his various incomprehensible notes and ineffective aides-mémoires that were generally left scattered around his office.

Finally, he chanced upon a recent tabloid newspaper hidden underneath an empty pizza box that fell open onto a small article about Lottie, and this prompted his memory, which was good timing as Lottie had just about grunted and wheezed her way to the top of the stairs.

"Well, Lottie! *Just* the person I wanted to speak to! Let's skip the formalities and get right to business, shall we?" Teddy began, after waiting patiently for a few minutes while a red-faced and rain-sodden Lottie finally caught her breath. "We need to have a serious discussion about your future as a... Well, you've had a career as a... I mean... Alright, for the sake of argument let's just call you a *public figure.* You're obviously aware that we've been struggling lately to keep marketing you as some kind of legitimate celebrity that people are still interested in. The various reality TV shows have been keeping us going for the past few years, but unfortunately the offers have all but dried up now. The one thing I advised you to do before was to try and get a bit more attention as I can barely get people interested in fake rumours about you anymore, and to be fair to you, the appearance on *Women's Natter* did just that".

Lottie winced at the mere mention of that wretched television show. She was still trying to forget about her recent disastrous live TV appearance, but the general public didn't seem willing to let her forget just yet.

"Your little on air rant at Stefani just as she announced her pregnancy has certainly damaged your reputation though, and Mrs O's unfortunate mispronunciation of your name has sadly made you a bit of a laughing stock. I'm sure that you've seen all the latest Internet memes and jokes by now".
"Not really", Lottie lied, unconvincingly.
"Me neither", he lied, guiltily.

Lottie had seen them all and so had Teddy. He secretly thought they were mostly hilarious, although even he knew better than to admit this to his troubled client. He cleared his throat and continued, "Unfortunately Lottie, you don't have a lot of support from the public here. Reality TV stars don't generally have a lot of proper fans because there's nothing tangible to be a fan of. Reality TV is what you make when the budget is too small to hire scriptwriters and the subject is too boring to make a documentary out of it. It's good for short-term exposure but it doesn't give you a meaningful fan base in the true sense of the word. Frankly, since that farce of an interview on *Women's Natter*, people are definitely noticing you again, but the big BUT here is that they really don't like you. As with everything in your life, there's always a big *But!*"

"Are you saying *but* or *butt*?" Lottie asked, suspiciously. She had long been subjected to what could generously be called Teddy's sense of humour and she knew the way his mind worked.

"Ha ha – exactly!" came his deliberately non-committal response. Then, as though working on autopilot, he took a biro pen from behind his ear and unthinkingly wrote '*Big <u>Butt</u>!*' on the nearest piece of paper in front of him. Even he wouldn't be able to explain why he had written it when he would find the note several days later.

Lottie was depressed. This couldn't have been more obvious unless she had announced it with an elaborate song and dance routine. She sighed heavily with a sad expression of down beaten weariness that was impossible to ignore and her shoulders sagged dramatically. It occurred to Teddy that she had put on even more weight lately, and this only served to heighten the dramatic effect of her deflated posture. He began to feel quite sorry for Lottie at that moment, which was a rather unusual feeling for him and something he rarely experienced in a professional capacity. As a general rule, Teddy had never formed much of a personal attachment to any of his clients but he had been working as Lottie's agent for some years now, ever since she had first left the reality TV house that had made her a household name, and he had gradually grown quite fond of her over their time together. She was, by and large, a quite good natured and amenable soul, even at the height of her notoriety and fame, and although her head might still be in the clouds a little bit, it was nothing compared to all the monstrous egomaniacs and self-entitled divas that Teddy had encountered throughout his long career in showbiz puppeteering.

"So what are you saying, Teddy? Am I *over*? Is there *anything* I can do to get people interested in me again and turn public opinion around?" Lottie asked, pleadingly.

Until that very moment, Teddy had been fully prepared to tell Lottie that her public persona was just about beyond redemption and that there wasn't really any potential in her as marketable public figure anymore. But the touchingly pathetic sight of Lottie trying to pretend she wasn't still out of breath from climbing all the stairs, the sad image of the woman finally coming to terms with being on the brink of obscurity and the sheer force of the hopeless desperation in her eyes caught Teddy off guard momentarily, and this made him do something that he had never done before, and would never do again. He changed his mind!

"Well... look, I've got a very good friend over at *Celebs Today* magazine. He knows the tabloid industry better than anyone I know, and he's helped to create quite a few household names over the years just by giving them the right kind of publicity at the right time. He's an editor and he really understands how the public thinks. If anybody can help you out, *he* is the man! I'll give him a call for you and see if I can set up a meeting between you both. In the meantime, well... maybe it's possible that you've milked the 'fat' aspect enough now, what do you think?"

A cautiously optimistic smile lit up Lottie's face, as she tried to ignore the well-meaning but clumsily worded observation about her weight and thanked him graciously. As she left, Teddy spent the next fifteen minutes skimming through various diaries, email conversations and ancient phonebooks, until he finally remembered what his 'very good friend' was actually called and found his phone number.

He picked up the phone and dialled the number. "David Paige!" Teddy chirped cheerfully down the phone when the call was answered, just as another loud attack of ferocious lightning lit up the dark sky outside his window, "*Just* the person I wanted to speak to!"

....

A few hours later, David Paige left his office at *Celebs Today* magazine and began to make his way home. It was a long walk, but it was still light out. David usually worked for such long hours that it had been quite a while since he had managed to leave the office while there was still daylight, but there was something different about today. It had technically also been several weeks since he had been home, too.

He hadn't remembered to bring an umbrella with him that morning, but instead becoming drenched by the heavy thunder and rain that David had been expecting to face on his evening walk home from work, he was happily surprised to find that by the time he left the office, the rain had stopped completely and the heavy, gloomy clouds had drifted off to find someone else's day they could ruin.

He almost began to feel as though the dismal dark storm clouds that were perpetually in his mind were slowly parting, allowing a little ray of much-needed light to break through, too.
There was a sense of change in the air and this was motivating him greatly today, defrosting his temperament and soothing his soul with hopeful, warming rays of unusually cheery sunshine.

Spring was coming. The days were becoming lighter and warmer. He was feeling more and more positive.

'Something'll probably come along to ruin it!' he instinctively thought to himself, but without much feeling this time. Even David's natural cynicism couldn't stifle his uncharacteristically good mood today, it seemed.

By his own admission, David was a fairly miserable soul who didn't have much faith in people and didn't see much beauty in this world. Bitter life experience had taught him that even if he felt as though good fortune was smiling upon him, something far more unpleasant would soon be heaped upon him before he actually had the chance to enjoy it. He wasn't just a 'glass half empty' kind of person. He was a 'glass half empty' kind of person who was always mentally prepared for someone to knock the glass out of his hand, spill the contents on his lap and hand him a bill for the pleasure. And, whether it was because of fate, pure bad luck or a simple case of a self-fulfilling prophecy, they invariably did just that.

However, in spite of his looming divorce, stifled career and insufferable boss, David was beginning to accept the conclusion that change was an inevitable part of life, and that if he could only change his attitude and perspective about the whole thing, then maybe that change could actually turn into a positive one for once.

After twenty-five minutes of walking in the early evening sunlight, which even David was now prepared to admit to himself wasn't entirely unpleasant; he finally arrived at his house. He ignored the fact that Angelica, his estranged-wife who had occupied their marital home alone since kicking him out a few weeks earlier, had seemingly disposed of his beloved garden gnomes and potted plants already. He had spent years collecting them. Angelica had always hated them and often scoffed that he liked his sad little collection of gnomes more than he liked people. David had felt that there was more than a hint of truth to this and was secretly a little baffled as to why this should even be considered odd. After all, no *gnome* had ever sought to ruin his day! However, he tried to ignore their glaring absence from what was still technically his home - he was determined to establish a more cordial and harmonious relationship with Angelica today no matter how much she provoked him.

"What do *you* want?" she demanded, poking her head out of an upstairs window before David had even knocked on the door.
"I've come to talk to you", David replied, arduously still trying to maintain the friendliest voice he was capable of.
"Talk to my lawyers!" she barked, and slammed the window shut.

David instantly felt his blood pressure rising and his almost-permanent scowl quickly re-established itself, burrowing deep into the well-worn grooves that were etched upon his face and chronicled years of misery - but still he fought against it. He was determined to maintain his cheerily optimistic new approach today, even if the effort caused him to have an aneurysm.

"Angelica! *Angelica!*" he shouted, painstakingly endeavouring not sound angry in spite of the circumstances. An interior light betrayed her presence in the room, highlighting her silhouette against the closed window as she hid behind the curtains. She was still there and still listening, even if she thought that she was out of sight. By the Paige's standards, this was progress at least.

"Look, I know that you can hear me so I'm just going to talk anyway. Angelica, I'm not here to fight with you, and I'm not going anywhere so you might as well listen to me. Angelica, this really is *ridiculous*! All these expensive lawyers and all this bitterness... it's just not necessary! I've tried to reconcile with you, and I've tried to fight with you. Neither of those things has worked out for me. You've *won*, Angelica! I'm prepared to walk away from this marriage if that's what you truly want, but *please* try to meet me half way at the very least!"

David squinted up at the window. Angelica was now openly staring down, directly at him. He finally had her attention. He persevered, embracing his overdue chance to speak more or less directly to her, face-to-window. "I feel I've been more than reasonable with you so far, and you've been offered what most people would consider to be a *very* generous divorce settlement already. Isn't that good enough? You can just have the car, and once the house has been sold I'm sure you'll be able to afford a perfectly nice little place of your own from your share of the proceeds. But taking the *dog*? Come on! That was just nasty! You know I love that dog. I understand that you technically registered him in your name when we spent that summer in New Zealand, but that doesn't justify you now using him as a bargaining tool just because you legally can! He's *my* dog, and you know it!"

There was still no response. The symbolic storm clouds were already starting to return in David's mind, gathering quickly and bringing with them an ominous new threat of thunder. He tried to ignore this. David swallowed his sense of injustice, swallowed his anger and prepared to swallow his pride as he continued. "Look, there's no sense in getting ugly about this! I *know things* about you, Angelica! I've put up with *far* more than any reasonable man should, and I'm *still* trying to meet you half way. Okay, fine! You can *have* the house! Just give me a break on the settlement and give me my dog back! We can work out a new deal. *Please*, Angelica! I won't beg... This is *more* than fair on you!"

Angelica disappeared from the window. '*Finally*', David thought to himself, as he tried to calm himself down and waited for the front door to open. He began to feel proud that he had resisted the urge to engage in a silly slanging match or an all-out war for once. And all it took was a little change in his attitude! Maybe you really do catch more flies with honey than with vinegar after all, he mused, feeling rather pleased with himself and guardedly relieved. He even allowed himself a relaxed smile. Suddenly, the upstairs window burst open again, and Angelica dropped a full bucket of ice-cold water directly onto David's head!

"Go away or I'll phone the police!" she snarled, slamming the window shut again.

As David trudged dejectedly through the streets back to the depressing hotel that he now called home, his feet squelched and squeaked mockingly with every step, and dark clouds formed in the sky again. It began to rain heavily once more.

His depressingly brief period of hopeful cheeriness had by now been wholly extinguished and irretrievably quenched. He had finally had enough. He had finally reached his long-overdue breaking point.

He took out his phone from his wringing wet pocket and made a futile effort to dry the screen against his equally sodden suit until he was able to call his lawyer's office.

Since it was out of office hours, David had to wait for the automated answering machine to put the call through to the lawyer's mobile phone. As he waited, David peculiarly began to think about an old reality TV star he had agreed to meet next week that had lately become a national figure of fun, thanks to her recent weight gain, some live TV disaster he was vaguely aware of and an unfortunate but comical mispronunciation of her name that had gone viral. A taunting inner thought occurred to David even *she* would have looked down her nose at him at that moment, as though even his subconscious was now mocking him.

He felt like the biggest loser in the whole world.

"Hello, it's David Paige here. I'm sorry to bother you so late. It's about my divorce", he announced as the lawyer finally answered his call, which immediately added another hour to David's ever-increasing invoice. "You asked in our last meeting whether my wife had ever been unfaithful to me…"

Lightning lit up the sky and there was another roar of thunder. David paused. His mind was suddenly working overtime. This could be a life defining moment for him. Maybe a change in attitude really *was* the way to go after all. Maybe he just needed a change in a different direction.

"Actually, never mind! Forget I called. Sorry for bothering you. Good night", David stammered apologetically as a dangerous and irresistible new idea suddenly began to form in his mind.

After all, if Angelica can take David's things away from him out of spite, then surely it was only fair and just that he should do the same to her.

Chapter Nine

"*Roger, this is Clive, your agent. You know how I prefer not to leave these voice messages, but you're obviously too busy doing something that I'd rather not know about to take my call. Or you've lost your phone again, which would actually be much worse, now that I come to think of it! Anyway, I'm calling to let you know that the man responsible for Cherlene's public divorce announcement and interview over at Celebs Today magazine has contacted me this morning, and he says that he wants to meet with you as soon as we can arrange it. If you remember any of my lectures about leaving sensitive information on mobile phones over the past six years, then you'll know why I can't say any more than that until I can speak to you directly. So please check your voicemail and call me back! Oh, and for the love of God, please make sure that you –* *End of message. Voicemail message box is full*"

Clive hung up the receiver and wondered why he even bothered to leave voice messages. Knowing Roger Scott as well as he did, he realised that there was only the remotest chance that his troubled client would ever hear it anyway. It was always far more likely that the messages would be heard by whichever random person found Roger's phone when he eventually lost it – which was always a fairly regular inevitability – or sold to some unscrupulous journalist and printed in the tabloids if the messages were deemed juicy enough. Roger had never been the most conscientious man when it came to his possessions, however sensitive they were. Clive had felt obliged to help Roger install a high-tech security entrance system in his house only one year before, to stop him from leaving his front door wide open whenever he left home, and Roger had still managed to lose his electronic entrance key no less than seven times since then. Still, Clive had very little option whenever Roger ignored his phone. It was either a voicemail message or an email, and Clive knew that there was *no* chance at all that Roger would ever check his emails even if he knew how to.

On the other side of London, Roger listened intently to the message his agent had left and then thought about it for a moment. He often wondered why Clive even bothered to leave voice messages, since Roger almost always pretended not to have heard them and Clive invariably rambled for so long that the voicemail settings usually cut him off before he had reached his main point anyway. This one sounded interesting though. Just over a week had passed since Cherlene's unexpected divorce petition, and the showbiz tabloids were still talking about little else. Why on earth would Clive even *want* Roger to meet the journalist-or-whomever that had helped Cherlene to humiliate him with that damning tabloid feature? Not only was it a lousy way to end a marriage, but it had also completely annihilated whatever fragments were left of Roger's already-shaky reputation. And more to the point, why on earth would the journalist want to meet with Roger anyway?

Even a slow moving, limited mind like Roger's could see what a bad idea it was that the two men should meet, but he also knew that Clive had an intellectual mind that was sharp and twisted like a corkscrew; especially when compared to Roger, who had a mind like a shrunken lump of cork. In short, Roger quickly reached the tried and tested conclusion that if Clive thought it was a good idea, then it was almost certainly a good idea.

Roger sat back in bed and turned to face his companion, who was lying partially clothed next to him and waiting for their informal date to formally begin. "I'm going to have to call my agent back and will probably be on the phone for a while, so maybe we should forget about today. In fact, I'm probably going to have to cool things between us altogether", he cautiously explained, speaking slowly and deliberately. Caution didn't come naturally to a man like Roger. Normally he would allow his words to just flow freely from his mouth, completely bypassing his brain and not remotely troubled by any taxing concepts such as tact, diplomacy or consequence, but today he was choosing his words very carefully indeed. He had given this matter some consideration over the past few days, which was also quite unusual for him. "I'm sorry but this divorce, the public shame, seeing my wife's pain and anguish printed clearly in black and

115

white... It's really made me think about things, prioritise my life and realise what's important". He paused dramatically for a few seconds, momentarily deep in thought at the importance of what he was about to say, before continuing, "I realise now that I'm going to have to take my public image much more seriously and stop wasting my time on these meaningless little flings. Otherwise, I may never get another paid sponsorship deal again!"

To Roger's mild surprise, his lover seemed to agree to this without so much as a token protest. He had been afraid of this part, as he had correctly come to suspect that the woman was far more besotted with him than she was letting on. "It's probably for the best", she conceded as she stood up and put her long designer trench coat on in one sweeping movement, "I am still a married woman, you know. I have a husband, and I have to think about my commitments and what I have to lose". Roger stared over her shoulder with a fixed expression for a moment, trying to work out whether he had actually forgotten that she was married or whether she had simply never mentioned it to begin with. She was almost out of the door as she added, "After all, if we were to be caught out with this fling, it could *really* jeopardise my divorce proceedings and eventual settlement pay-out. I have to think about what's important to me too. Bye!"

"Well, that was easy!" Roger smiled to himself as the door slammed behind his now *ex*-lover. "I just hope that all the others take the news so well", he added, picking up his phone and preparing to significantly reduce his number of casual lovers. But before he began a long afternoon of breaking hearts in a diplomatic, painless and hopefully swift kind of way, he called his agent back. Something about Clive's message suggested that there was something very important about this meeting, and for once, Roger actually wanted to learn more.

....

Phones were ringing incessantly. Computer keyboards were clattering relentlessly. People were cursing and arguing either with each other, cursing and arguing with themselves or cursing and arguing with the odd rage-inducing memo or uncooperative piece of office technology. To a casual observer, the noise level might be considered akin to several riots all occurring at the same time, and the ear-splitting audio backdrop was practically at the pain threshold from the moment you walked through the door, but to the people working at the busy offices of *Celebs Today* magazine headquarters, this was just another perfectly ordinary 'one-day-before-the-weekly-publication-deadline' frenzy. It was all part of the regular scheduled chaos that they had become accustomed to. Amid all the hustle and bustle, David's assistant took a phone call from a frantically apologetic, slightly breathless woman who sounded as though she might possibly be midway through running a marathon. "Hi, I'm Lottie Klünt. That's *Klünt*, as in *K-l-o-o-n-t*. I have an appointment to meet somebody called David Paige but I'm afraid I'm running a little late. Your security men won't let me into the car park. Isn't there *anywhere* to park around here?"

Nearly thirty minutes later, David and Lottie were sitting alone in his private office, safely shut off from the pandemonium just outside his door. They sat in silence as they waited for his assistant to bring them coffee, although this wasn't really necessary and David was secretly just waiting for Lottie to catch her breath after running from wherever she had hastily abandoned her car to the office, clearly eager not to keep him waiting any longer. He almost asked her how far away she had eventually parked, but tactfully stopped himself just in time. It occurred to him that although she sounded as though she had just run across several miles of rough terrain, Lottie also looked as though she was pretty much built out of pork and donuts, so he kindly pretended not to notice as she feebly pretended not to gasp for breath, and the two of them politely settled for pretending that they were waiting for the coffee instead.

Eventually, the hot beverages were brought to them. Lottie helped herself to several biscuits as David was finally able to begin.
"Let me start by saying that whatever we discuss today must stay between these four walls. That is to say, you

are not to tell *anyone* about this meeting. Don't text about it. Don't email about it. Don't write any notes in your calendars, diaries or computers etcetera. Careers more established and more stable than yours have been ruined by leaked info, hacked emails, lost notes, bugged telephones and so on, as I'm sure you must be aware of, so if you ever even think that you're being too careful, trust me, *you're not!*"

Lottie's eyes widened. This sounded interesting! She acknowledged the warning and agreed, although she was somewhat dubious that anyone would be interested enough in her life to bother reading her messages anyway. She could barely rouse enough interest for a staged photo opportunity anymore, even if she made the effort to organise it herself.

David went on. "I've spoken to your agent Teddy, and he's explained a bit about the situation you're in, professionally speaking. He seems to think I might be able to help you. I can. There's no doubt about it. I can help you. *But* – and this is a *Big BUT...*"

Lottie rolled her eyes, instinctively interpreting 'big but' as another cheap jibe about her weight.

"... I cannot stress the importance of this enough. This – Must – Be – One – Hundred – Percent – Secret!"

"Fine!" Lottie agreed, eager for David to begin explaining his plan for helping her.

"If we were to be publicly caught out with what I'm going to suggest, make no mistake, it would ruin your career *and* mine! And I'm sure I wouldn't be out of line to suggest that my career is far more important than yours. I actually *have* a career, for a start!"

"Yes, fine! I understand!" Lottie agreed, trying to mask her rapidly growing impatience with the man. What *was* his plan?

"I would even go as far as to suggest", David spoke slowly and cautiously, knowing full well that what he was about to ask of her was a tremendous price to pay, "... that you keep your agent Teddy out of the loop on this one. If you really, *really* want to be famous, that is? *Very* famous, I mean. I might even suggest that you break ties with him altogether". David braced himself, partially expecting an angry tirade from Lottie at this point at the sheer audacity of his suggestion.

"Fine!" she responded, without taking even a moment to think about it. "I'll ditch him this afternoon as soon as our meeting is over. Just please tell me, *how* can I become really, *really* famous!?"

David smiled. *This* was the type of person that made his job so much easier.

"Before I answer that, let me ask you a question. How much do you know about a footballer called Roger Scott?"

....

"He wants you to do *what?*" Clive asked his client, aghast.
Roger explained the plan again.
Clive listened intently. He thought about it some more. He drummed his fingers on the desk thoughtfully. He cleared his throat as though contemplating something important. He picked up one of the tabloid magazines in front of him and stared at it quizzically. Eventually, he heard the click of the wall clock indicate that it was now two o'clock, but this time, instead of making a mental note to invoice his client for another hour - taking his typical viewpoint that even a minute past the hour could be technically billed as another full hour's work – he simply asked Roger to explain David's plan once again. This was good. This was *really* good. Clive wouldn't have dared to admit this to anyone – mainly because good PR wasn't *just* for the clients when it came to being a celebrated 'PR guru' - but even *he* wouldn't have dreamed up such a cynical, brilliantly dastardly plan to salvage Roger's public image and career. But, as crazy as it sounded, it just *might* work.

Whoever David Paige was, Clive mused, he must have a very special way of thinking that was either utterly wasted in tabloid journalism, or utterly *perfect* for it!

....

"Explain this to me one more time", Lottie repeated, thoroughly aghast. "You want me to do *what?*"

"*Diet!*" David answered, bluntly.

"Yes, yes. We covered *that* part", Lottie exclaimed, irritably, "You've made that point quite well, thank you. I was more concerned with the part of the plan where I pretend to get *engaged* to Roger Scott, then pretend to break up with him in public by accusing him of cheating on me, and then pretend to have a massive row about it even though he hasn't and it's all been a sham romance from the start?!"

"Well, that's basically it", David answered, in the manner of one trying to explain that two plus two really does equal four and entirely failing to understand the other person's incomprehension.

David's idea, as he presented it, was an elaborate public ruse in the form of a volatile celebrity relationship breakup that would eventually redefine how the general public saw both Lottie and Roger, provide David's career with a real shot in the arm by giving *Celebs Today* a front row seat to the entire debacle, and most crucially for Lottie, put her in the headlines again and squeeze her firmly back into the spotlight. It could be a win, win, win situation for all of them, he explained.

Part of Lottie thought that David's plan was preposterously absurd, as though spending far too much time working by himself in dark offices for the tabloid magazines had left him viewing the concept of celebrity as some kind of convoluted soap opera with real life characters that he could control and manipulate. Part of her thought that David's breezy explanation sounded altogether too easy, as though anybody who had the audacity to try to take part in such a cynically staged 'show-mance' would undoubtedly be caught out and would surely deserve all the vast amounts of humiliation and ridicule that the world could inflict upon them.

There was an unceasingly cold, calm logic to David's demeanour that was neither alarming nor comforting and therefore seemed virtually impossible to read. Lottie tried to meet his gaze and just couldn't decide whether she saw a bold genius or a raving madman staring back at her. But there were many parts of Lottie to spare, and the largest part of her screamed, *'I don't care how he does it, but here is a man who can make me very, very famous!'*

123

Not just famous, but also significantly richer once Lottie mentally factored in all the interviews, TV appearances, photo shoots and magazine feature opportunities that a celebrity engagement could bring. For those who wanted it, being rich and being famous pretty much amounted to the same thing; it didn't even really matter which of the two came first, you only needed to know how to successfully exploit being one before you also became the other. And Lottie *did* want it. She wanted to be known as the famous girl stealing the spotlight, not just the hefty girl blocking the sunlight.

The more she turned it over in her mind, the more it was beginning to make sense for her. But that in itself brought up another troubling point. Being one part of this proposed celebrity engagement and subsequent breakup only seemed to make sense for *her*.

"And this guy Roger has *actually* agreed to this sham engagement and breakup already?" Lottie exclaimed. This was the one part that she really couldn't understand. If this adulterous former footballer Roger Scott wanted to restore his broken reputation, why on earth would he ever agree to be the villain in this phoney public pantomime?

David explained the plan again.

Chapter Ten

Lottie saw the looming northern entrance of Blackfriars railway station in the distance and swore, realising that she had walked in a complete loop again. How many times was that now, she wondered? Three? Four? She had been circling the area for almost an hour trying to remember where she had last seen her own car, which she had once again hastily abandoned in whatever random space it could squeeze into before her meeting with David. Lottie blundered and ambled her way through the streets in an absent-minded daze, while the part of her conscious mind that normally paid attention to important things - such as where she currently was and where she was actually going - remained almost entirely preoccupied with other matters.

Eventually, Lottie rounded a corner and was relieved to finally recognise the hidden side street that she had parked in earlier that afternoon. She recognised her car, parked in its typical fashion, which was clumsily half mounted on the pavement and facing the wrong direction in a one-way street. She wasn't at all surprised to recognise the familiar unwelcome sight of yet another bright yellow parking ticket on her windscreen.

Then, before she had even reached the car, Lottie herself was also recognised by a couple of passersby in the street, one of whom she clearly overheard commenting loudly to the other, "There's that fat one who used to do reality TV and sexy lads' mag photos. Hasn't she let herself go?"

Lottie huffily pulled the parking fine off her windscreen. She seemed to be more popular with London's traffic wardens than anyone else in the whole country right now. Her Dad often liked to joke that it would probably be cheaper for her to buy her own personal multi-storey car park than pay all the fines she regularly acquired. At least, Lottie assumed that he was joking.

A rowdy group of early evening drinkers staggered out of a nearby bar, and one or two of them recognised Lottie too. They didn't know exactly who she was, but they had apparently seen a video clip of her much-ridiculed appearance on *Women's Natter*. That much was obvious. They taunted her from across the street, jeering loudly and deliberately mispronouncing her name in the same crude way that Mrs O mistakenly had in that now-infamous live TV gaffe. Lottie put her head down and unconvincingly pretended not to notice them as she kept on walking, acting as though she was the only person on the busy street who somehow couldn't hear the obnoxious drunken heckling. It was humiliating. She *hated* how people reacted to her nowadays. She had always liked being famous, but it never used to be like this. It had felt different before. Where had the adoration gone? The fans? The support? Everyone deserved their fifteen minutes of fame, she lamented, and the first few minutes were almost always electrifying and addictive, but those final few minutes were usually the worst of all. Lottie simply wasn't ready to give it all up just yet.

Once she had walked out far enough to be out of the drunken hecklers' sight, Lottie ducked into a small bar, ordered herself a large glass of wine and sat quietly in the corner, accompanied only by her thoughts and enjoying the relative quiet of the drab surroundings. Nobody seemed to be paying her much attention in here. She didn't notice the barman's lingering stare as he had tried to work out where he recognised her familiar face from, nor did she notice his breezy shrug of indifference a moment later, as he mentally dismissed the idea that she might be a former romantic conquest and quickly lost interest.

The lights were switched on for the evening. A few more people entered the bar. The bartender targeted his next potential romantic conquest and somebody turned on the jukebox. Lottie managed to ignore all of this, staring distantly at nothing in particular and enjoying nothing more than her own company. Sometimes you didn't need the glitz and glamour of a showbiz event or exclusive nightclub, Lottie thought to herself. Sometimes all you needed was to be left alone with your thoughts and a nice glass of wine.

Disappointingly, Lottie ran out of both of these after just a couple of minutes. She asked for a refill – just in time to overhear the barman completely failing to seduce an attractive patron by overconfidently boasting, "Of course I'm not married! Why settle for an old *'Saggy Naggy'* wife when I could meet a new *'Busty Lusty'* like you every night of the week?" – and sat back down. As she idly glanced around for something more interesting to look at than a sleazy barman who somehow seemed to be both full of himself and extremely lacking at the same time, Lottie noticed some dog-eared reading materials that the pub had left out for its customers. She glanced at a few of them. They were mostly ghost-written autobiographies and sordid kiss-and-tell publications. Lottie skimmed through some of the titles, like 'Sex, Drugs & Reality TV', 'Why We Will Never Get Back Together Again', 'Lying Lips & Fake Orgasms', 'He Touched My Heart & He Touched My Friends', 'My Journey Of Fake Boobs & Other Betrayals', 'Hollywood's Best Colonoscopy Secrets Revealed' and other such nonsense, and even *she* failed to recognise half of the so-called celebrity authors whose names were on the covers. One of them was a middle-aged French-Canadian woman calling herself Lucille D'Amour, whose only claim to fame, according to the cover, was that she had been a makeup artist to most of the actors she was claiming to have had liaisons with. Clearly there was quite a lucrative market out there for Z-lister celebrities and their doomed romances.

A recent copy of *Celebs Today* magazine had also been left out on a nearby table. Roger and Cherlene Scott's divorce still dominated most of the celebrity tabloid headlines, in spite of the fact that there seemingly hadn't been any actual developments since the split had been announced. Cherlene was really milking this newfound attention for all it was worth, whereas Roger almost appeared to have gone into hiding. He was very much being portrayed as the villain in this tabloid tale.

Although Lottie had been determined not to dwell too much on it, she finally gave up and reflected on her meeting with David earlier that afternoon. She rehashed his suggested 'fake relationship' plan over and over in her mind again.

David had everything all planned out. Roger had apparently already agreed with David earlier in the week to take part in the charade, and by the end of the afternoon, so had Lottie. She and Roger would pretend to be in a loving relationship with one another. For the first part of the charade, they would spend weeks posing as a couple enjoying romantic dinners together, taking little trips with each other and pretending to be 'caught' by the paparazzi generally being loved-up and amorous with one another. After a few weeks of this, they would finally confirm their relationship with a big magazine feature interview - exclusive to *Celebs Today*, naturally - and then once Roger's marriage to Cherlene was formally dissolved, he and Lottie would even announce their own engagement. This would be sure to guarantee them countless headlines and a lot of exposure coming so soon after Roger's high profile divorce, and obviously, *Celebs Today* would already be guaranteed the exclusive interviews and photographs every step of the way. None of this was especially unusual. Roger and Lottie wouldn't be the first fame-hungry celebrities to engage in a sham romance and they certainly wouldn't be the last.

"Trust me, I could name a lot of megastars and A-listers who have done this type of thing before", David had told Lottie. "You'd be surprised by how many sham marriages there are out there in Hollywood even to this day, and lots of people know it. It's a bit of an open secret when you work in the tabloid industry. They all get away with it as well, because how you could actually prove otherwise? I could tell you some names of celebs who are in sham marriages, just between us, but you certainly couldn't publish their names in a book or something or you would almost certainly be sued".

Since it was just the two of them and there was nobody around to overhear, write about or repeat what was being said, David named some names. He was right. Lottie *was* very surprised.

The second part of David's plan, however, was where things took a surprising turn. David had explained his idea that Roger and Lottie would eventually end their relationship and engagement with one explosive dramatic showdown – somewhere nice and public where there could be lots of witnesses and, crucially, lots of photographers - under the pretence that Lottie suddenly caught her notoriously fickle new fiancé cheating on her with another woman. She would confront him somewhere very public, and then he would spinelessly run off into the night, leaving his devastated fiancé humiliated and broken-hearted. Lottie – after making the most of a few priceless photo opportunities for the crowds and photographers who had witnessed the confrontation, of course - would chase after him, showing herself to be a heartbroken but fiery woman scorned. Photographers working for *Celebs Today* would already be waiting at Roger's house before she arrived, giving them the advantage to get the exclusive juicy snaps of her arrival at the house for a second explosive confrontation. Once here, there would be an easy opportunity for 'one of the neighbours' to make an anonymous phone call to the police – perhaps David would do this himself - who would then quickly arrive to investigate reports of a domestic disturbance and indirectly provide the baying paparazzi even more exciting photo opportunities.

As David had explained, Lottie would make the headlines like never before. This would be worth more column inches than any amount of crap television shows or staged photos of her unsightly beach body, he insisted. If they managed to handle the breakup and especially the fiery confrontation well enough, they might even make the national news. It could be tabloid gold! Afterwards, Lottie could talk about her relationship with Roger, the bitter breakup and the unforgettable altercation for months and months, spilling headline-worthy anecdotes and juicy details on all the chat shows and in all magazines. She would be a social media trend. She would quickly become the hottest candidate for all the newest reality TV shows again. She could truly milk it for all its worth.

"The press just love a 'woman scorned'", David had told her, convincingly.

Lottie was impressed. David had seemingly thought of every meticulous detail and eventuality. "Anybody can call the police and report an altercation. It's free. The police will come and no charges will be pressed against anybody. But our paps will be waiting and will capture every moment of the drama. We'll just say it was a mistake afterwards. No harm, no foul. Everybody wins!"

But one question had still remained.

"So why Roger Scott? Why on earth would he agree to any of this?" Lottie had asked, genuinely perplexed. "*Me*, I can understand. I can make a lot of money from these interviews if people are interested enough, and it certainly won't do me any harm to be remembered for something more than being *that fat girl who used to be thin and was accidently called a you-know-what on TV*. There's no such thing as bad publicity, at least as far as I'm concerned! *You*? That's obvious. You get your exclusive stories, the best pictures, the first interviews and all that stuff. But *Roger*? His football career is over, and if his reputation has been ruined now by the cheating-on-his-wife scandal, why the hell would he ever agree to *pretend* to cheat on someone else?"

"Let's just say that even for a dumb failed footballer, he's always been the wettest pebble on the beach", David had shrugged dismissively. Lottie couldn't help but notice that there seemed to be some genuine feeling behind this statement. David realised that Lottie was clearly expecting more of a substantial explanation.

"I spoke with Roger and we both agreed that we should use his dodgy reputation to his advantage. He's a womaniser. Pure and simple. Ask any man on the street and that's exactly what they'll tell you. There's no escaping that anymore and there's no use in pretending that he is anything else. One way to counter this is to *turn into the skid*, so to speak. After you and he stage your breakup, he will enter a rehab facility claiming to be suffering from sex addiction. He'll acknowledge his faults, make his apologies and actively seek to improve himself, or at least as far as the general public knows, anyway. That way, when he re-emerges from rehab, he can promote himself as a completely rehabilitated character with a clean slate. He'll also then be able to do a load of magazine features and TV interviews about how he nobly overcame his addiction, which'll make him a shed load of money and establish him as a reformed man. Y'know, a sort of underdog you can really root for,

133

rather than plunging into obscurity and being remembered mostly for being Cherlene Scott's cheating ex-husband".

"So, the point is..?"

"The point is that his marriage breakdown has really hurt his reputation and marketability quite badly this time. His ex, Cherlene, wants to use all the attention that the divorce is bringing to become a big public figure herself. She'll drag his name through the mud to do so. He wants to divert attention from her and make it all about him again. *He wants to take the power back*". David paused momentarily, as though this thought suddenly distracted him with a different, more unwelcome thought. He quickly dismissed whatever had caused the brief interruption and continued; "One ex-WAG can make a name for herself just by riding on the coattails of a notorious scandal. But if there's more than one, then they're sort of lumped together and *he* becomes the centre of the story again. The public are fickle like that. It's one of the few things you can count on".

Lottie had still looked unconvinced. "There's no point in trying to make sense of it", David shrugged dismissively. "I'm sure that you've heard the expression; *all is fair in love and war*".

Lottie had considered this for a moment. Surely that couldn't be right? She was vaguely aware from sort of an outsider perspective that breakups and divorces often became a pretty complicated business, especially once a person's emotions overtook their logic and rationality. But surely the limits that one would go to just for the sake of some petty power struggle in a soured relationship wouldn't stretch *this* far? No, she had decided. David was wrong about that. He had to be. Divorces were costly. Roger was probably just interested in all the money that could be made by those who were willing to exploit the general public's interest in a celebrity's personal life, and that was all there was to it.

A tiny internal voice of reason warned that Lottie might be potentially straying into unfamiliar emotional territory, but the alluring glare of the promised spotlight at the end of a very dark tunnel of obscurity quickly overshadowed whatever tiny reservations remained. The opportunity to be making headlines again and to have people rooting for her was just far too tempting to pass up. Besides, in spite of his quiet, unassuming and frankly somewhat charmless demeanour, Lottie had been left with the strong impression that David was still a devilishly intelligent man underneath. He had repeatedly and emphatically assured her that his secret plan could work brilliantly for all concerned, so long as they all played their respective roles and never betrayed their secret. Lottie didn't detect so much as a flicker of doubt in the man.

He probably did this kind of thing all the time, she reassured herself.

More importantly though, just eight of David's words were still repeating over and over like a broken record in Lottie's mind ever since he had casually uttered them earlier. "If you want to be really, *really* famous"...

She really, *really* did.

"Okay, I'm on board!" she had announced after they had discussed all of this. "So, how do we actually convince people that Roger and I are in a romantic relationship?"

"That's simple", David smiled calmly in response. "We'll start the rumour the easiest way I know how to get a rumour started... We'll *deny* it!"

Chapter Eleven

David leaned back in his creaky, well-worn office chair and stared idly out of the window, silently observing the lights and the busy activities of the city below without taking much of an active interest. People are often said to be lost in a sea of thoughts during moments of quiet contemplation like this, but this poetic idiom wasn't entirely appropriate for a mind as cynically controlled as David's.

David rarely became lost in his own thoughts. He mapped and *navigated* them. It was just in the world outside his head where things generally became trickier. Perhaps people were just too busy *living* their own lives to bother stopping and observing them. But for someone whose only major success in life was a career essentially built on observing the more interesting lives that other people were living, it often seemed to David that people just didn't seem to think about things in the same way that he did.

He barely noticed the approaching footsteps coming towards his office, nor the gentle, almost-apologetic knock on the door. He didn't register anything outside of his mind's eye until a sudden voice startled him. "Are you okay in there, Mr Paige?"

"Hmm? What? Oh, yes, everything's fine. Am I the last

one here again?" David wearily asked, already knowing what the answer would be.

"I'm 'fraid so, Mr Paige. I'm going to get myself a coffee after I've done my security checks. Shall I fetch you one?"

"No thanks..." David searched his memory banks for the night guard's name, "...*Dereck*, isn't it? I'll just tidy up these papers then I'll call it a night".

"Right you are, Mr Paige. I'll check in again in half an hour, just in case. Oh, and my name's *David*, by the way. Just like *yours*, Mr Paige".

David winced inwardly at his mistake. Failing to remember a person's name when you had crossed paths at work almost every night for the past few years was probably considered impolite at the very least. But failing to remember a person's name when they shared the exact same name as you probably sounded like a very deliberate and meaningful slight. Even though he was aware that he wasn't one, David (Paige) had always at least *tried* to be a people person. He just never seemed able to get the right people. Or maybe it was he that was somehow the wrong person.

It was nearly a quarter to eleven already. Night time seemed to creep up on David now that he had nowhere in particular to go. He sighed, and decided to take one last look through the gossip columns on his desk before he went back to the soulless hotel that had been his home for far too long now. Like a mad scientist working in his laboratory, an explosion of documents, calendars, tabloid magazines and newspapers surrounded him. He muttered to himself as he breezily skimmed through some of the smaller gossip items, summarising each story he read under his breath with his own dead beat indifference: "*Some movie star pretends to enjoy working with her known rival on their latest movie together* – pity she's such a bad actress or I might have actually believed her… *Quiz show host appears tired and emotional leaving a hotel bar* – well that's obvious tabloid code for drunk… *Reality TV singing competition winner covers classic song at award show… blah, blah, blah… Four people die of internal haemorrhaging* – She's such an utterly atrocious singer, there even might be an unwritten connection between those last two stories".

By the time David had finished scanning the all the tabloids, he found what he had been looking for. Two of the tabloids had printed tiny, brief, blink-and-you'd-miss-it mentions of Lottie Klünt.

"*Reality TV star Lottie Klünt updates her TwitchFace page to deny rumours that she is dating recently separated ex-footballer Roger Scott*", David read from the bottom of one gossip page, mildly disappointed at the lack of column inches or sanctimonious tone.
The next tabloid offered a more promising depiction though: "*Shamed footballer Roger Scott found himself embroiled in another scandal this week, as rumours circulate that he is now dating former Reality TV star*

Lottie Klünt. Coming just weeks after his wife Cherlene Scott shockingly announced that she is set to divorce him following years of adultery, the troubled star is said to have already grown close to the former lads' mag pinup, and his concerned friends are threatening to stage an intervention".

David was pleased. So far, Lottie had only done what David had told her to do, which was to post a public message on her official social media page *denying* any rumours that she was dating Roger Scott. There were no rumours, obviously, but David was hoping that at least someone would take the bait and *believe* that there were rumours – whether or not they believed that they were actually true at this stage was largely irrelevant – and report them as gossip. The fact that they had been reported, embellished and exaggerated in the press already was just the icing on the cake. The little detail about Roger's friends threatening to intervene was perfect – this was the type of pure fabricated tabloid fodder that fuelled these non-stories, and it was precisely what David had been hoping for. This was laughably easy. Things were already going exactly according to the plan.

David sat back in his squeaky chair and thought about the coming weeks. He even came close to allowing himself a satisfied smile. Suddenly, an unexpected voice startled him once again.

"Are you still okay in there, Mr Paige? It's a quarter past

eleven now, and I'm just doing my security rounds again. Are you not going home at all tonight? Shall I fetch you a coffee or something?"

....

Over the next few weeks, both Lottie and Roger individually followed David's instructions closely, and more and more rumours slowly began to circulate that they were dating. Firstly, Lottie posted a couple of public denials responding to non-existent rumours about their budding new romance. Once this had been mentioned in a couple of gossip columns, she waited a few days before writing about Roger again, now subtly confirming they were spending time together in an indirect way by claiming that they were "just good friends". This time, Roger publically replied to her social media update with a message of his own, thanking her for her support throughout his difficult times and calling her a "wonderful person". David insisted on secretly writing Roger's social media posts himself. The hardest part was simply remembering to include the spelling mistakes and poor grammar, lest anyone get wind of the fact that Roger was not actually the man writing them.

Hundreds of thousands of people following Roger Scott's official TwitchFace profile could see this response, and this quickly began to attract a lot more attention to the hearsay. David further roused the public's interest when he encouraged a TV presenter that he knew to ask Cherlene Scott directly whether she was aware of Lottie's rumoured romance with her estranged husband in a live televised interview. She denied any knowledge of the rumours, of course – it was important that Cherlene knew nothing about the sham romance plan – but merely acknowledging the tittle-tattle in front of a large audience of television viewers firmly planted the story into public consciousness.

Phase One appeared to be completed just as David had anticipated. The tabloids had caught the scent of a budding new story, and people were now beginning to take an interest on their own.

Lottie leisurely sauntered into the billowing white reception area of Pandora's Box and kindly approached the receptionist. "Hi, I'm Lottie Klünt – that's *K-l-o-o-n-t*. I have a three o'clock appointment, although I'm probably a little early", she proudly announced with a relaxed smile.

"Actually, you're almost six minutes late", the harsh-faced receptionist sternly responded, extending a mostly acrylic finger towards the wall clock like the worst kind of headmistress. What she lacked in facial expression, she more than made up for in her lack of friendly tone. "Take a seat over there and wait. Luckily for you, Pandora is running a little behind on her appointments today anyway. We're very full today with appointments".

"*Pandora?*" Lottie asked, bemused.
"Yes. Is there a problem?" the humourless receptionist demanded.
"The woman I am meeting today, the woman who runs Pandora's Box, is actually *called* Pandora*?*"
"Yes. Pandora opened Pandora's Box eight months ago. Lots of people use Pandora's Box. *Is there something amusing you, Miss Klünt!?*"
"No, not at all!" Lottie stammered, like a naughty schoolgirl completely failing to stifle an involuntary giggle. "I'll just go wait over here then, shall I?"

Lottie sat down and waited. She waited and waited and waited. *'How typical'*, she thought to herself after a while, *'I thought I'd be sensible and book a taxi for once, even timing it so I'd get here twenty minutes before I needed to; the taxi turns up apparently almost twenty-six minutes late, and now that I'm finally here, Pandora's far too busy to squeeze me into her famous 'box' on time anyway!"*

Eventually, Lottie was ushered into the plush office and finally met the infamous Pandora. Pandora – who Lottie wouldn't have been entirely surprised to learn was using a professional alias and was actually called Agnes Cradge – was a high profile, highly strung and hugely

expensive image consultant who had been recommended to Lottie to give her a much-needed makeover and completely overhaul her image.
Everything about her appeared to be razor sharp, from her hips to her cheekbones to her pointy shoes. She even had long, ironing-board-straight hair that looked so perfectly sculpted, as though not a single follicle had the audacity to dare step out of place. She also appeared to have attended the same school of charm as her ghastly charmless receptionist.

In spite of this, Lottie had to admit to herself that the woman was explicitly beautiful. She had the type of personality that would make even a plastic shop mannequin appear warm and cuddly, but she also had the kind of appearance that could make the same mannequin look at itself in the mirror, and wish it could lose ten pounds and have smoother skin.

Pandora had many high-profile clients, she boasted, and there were many photos of some of the women she had dressed displayed around her office. Lottie looked at a few of them curiously while the razor-sharp Pandora talked vividly about colours, contouring and focal points, all the time dropping little vicious hints about various cosmetic surgeries that one might consider. She walked around Lottie in circles, wincing occasionally like a mechanic who is about to take on a *big* and costly job, all the while talking at length about Lottie's features; how best to enhance them, which bits could be hidden, which

bits should be removed completely and which bits they could simply draw attention away from.
By the end, it appeared that there was very little of Lottie left worth keeping.

"Basically, you're too fat", the £400-an-hour image consultant concluded after almost exactly an hour.

"Well I'd pretty much reached that conclusion for myself", Lottie huffily responded, "In fact, my mirror gives me the same advice for *free* every single morning when I get dressed!"

"Oh, don't feel *bad* though, you poor old thing!" Pandora enthused, drastically changing her tone and suddenly keen to sound as warm and pleasant as possible, lest she lose what could turn out to be a very profitable client. She flashed Lottie a dazzlingly bright smile and attempted to pat her shoulder in what she inexpertly hoped was a friendly manner. Pandora clearly wasn't used to smiling much in her profession. She probably felt that she couldn't afford the potential wrinkles. She went on, "There are always options available for those who really need - I mean, of course, those who really *want* to reinvent themselves, and I'll never shy away from a challenge however small or... erm... otherwise. Like I always say to my clients, there's nothing too *flabby*, *saggy* or *baggy* that Pandora's Box can't fix, hide or colour!"

Lottie relaxed a bit. "I suppose I do have a bit of an overactive knife and fork", she shamefully admitted with half-hearted joviality. "Mostly, I just want to feel desirable again. I used to wake up feeling like a million dollars. Now I just wake up feeling like – "

"...insufficient funds?" Pandora suggested, habitually unable to stifle the nasty comment.

"*Anyway*", Lottie thundered on, ignoring the remark, "I guess I gradually grew tired of trying to live up to the sexy glamour model image I had created. But now that it's really gone, I find that I'm actually more tired of just trying to find clothes that fit me without leaving a bruise. Frankly, I'm tired of feeling like even my birthday suit is poised to burst at the seams!"

"Yes, I can *completely* see what you mean", the razor-sharp Pandora instantly agreed without so much as a courteous hesitation. "Well, let's start with your hair and work our way down, shall we? But before we do anything else, how about I reschedule my next two appointments and we'll do something about those eyebrows? Wax them... shave them... *mow* them – they simply *have* to go!"

Lottie left two hours later, eight hundred pounds lighter, and with slightly different eyebrows.

Chapter Twelve

Regular readers of tabloid magazines, showbiz sections in newspapers, gossip websites and other such mediums will eventually come to recognise certain patterns in the stories being reported, and learn to spot certain tell-tale signs in the behaviour of their idols. Famous people typically pay little heed to false rumours and stories about themselves – they are considered to be par for the course by those in the spotlight and the fake rumours usually die down within a week or two if no-one gives them too much attention anyway. However, celebrity couples – for example - who might be genuinely experiencing hardships in their private relationships will often go to great lengths to *publicly* demonstrate how happy and committed they are to one another, lest anyone believe any stories to the contrary. Typically, this involves joint public appearances, gushing interviews, family days out that the paparazzi just happen to be there to witness and sickeningly sweet public displays of affection; it usually fools no-one and often only serves to confirm the rumours in the minds of anyone paying attention to such antics. Likewise, when two celebrities going about their regular business away from the spotlight happen to be in the same unlikely place together – finding themselves on the same flight, waiting in line at the same coffee house or shopping in the same store – it is usually a harmless opportunity for the stars to gain a mildly interesting anecdote about one another that they can talk about in their next interview, or even a nice photo opportunity that would be sure to be a big hit on their social media accounts. Assuming, of course, that their chance encounter was in fact a happy coincidence. Tabloid readers often love to see through the cheesy fake smiles of those who cannot bear to let their obvious rivalry get in the way of a good photo opportunity, especially if it comes with a delightful *damning with faint praise* kind of compliment.

The opposite of this occurs when two celebrities happen to be in the same place at the same time and are clearly going to great lengths to *avoid* being photographed together; even the most casual observer will likely reach the conclusion that they probably have either a bitter feud or something romantic to hide.

People always try to read between the lines when it comes to celebrity gossip, and they always like to guess and speculate about the stories that they're *not* being told, far more than they give credence to the edited narrative being sold.

It had always amazed David Paige that more celebrities hadn't learned how to control and take advantage of this. The public were incredibly easy to manipulate once you realised and finally accepted that they weren't *remotely* interested in what any celebrities actually had to say – it was always so much more interesting to find out what celebrities were trying to *hide* instead!

It was early evening. *The Hole In The Wall* – a rather rowdy and fairly tawdry nightclub on the outskirts of Brixton – was gearing up for another busy Saturday night. Its ageing décor, backstreets location and grim reputation didn't exactly give the impression of a lively hot spot of sophisticated entertainment, but its notoriously cheap drink promotions, late opening hours and lack of dress code requirements ensured that it regularly welcomed many patrons through its doors – often when they had been turned away from other, more selective establishments.

The overall ambience of the place relied on the questionable principle that dim lighting was all that was required to disguise the chipped paint on the walls, the ominous stains on the floor and the cheap furnishings that its customers occasionally stumbled into or attacked one another with.
Its tastelessness was such that on some strange level it essentially became its virtue. There could be no outfit too tacky, no behaviour too debauched and no liaison too shameless that would evoke judgement from anyone choosing to spend their evening in a place like *The Hole In The Wall*.

Or to put it another way, it was the type of place that made you want to wipe your feet on the way *out*.

An outside observer might have noted that the ladies' lavatories arguably seemed to be the most popular room in the entire establishment, providing a harshly lit but private place for women to gather, gossip, reapply their makeup, take endless photos of one another or engage in other more secretive activities away from the generic, bass-heavy racket that the DJ was inflicting on the main bar.
The gents' facilities, by contrast, provided an unwelcome and dangerous game of *'Who can make it to the urinals without getting their ankles wet?'*

A solitary security man manned the entrance while his fellow bouncers bounced around inside the noisy club. This particular nightclub bouncer often stood guard alone on the main door; it was a position he very much considered the short straw of the job, as he wanted to be inside where the action invariably was. The problem, as he saw it, was that he had so little to actually do here. The club had no dress code for him to sternly enforce, no exclusive guest list for him to slowly check with painstaking care and an unyielding air of suspicion; disappointingly, he wasn't even allowed to force people to queue up and respect his authority for a short while before letting them enter. Even when anything exciting enough happened that a customer needed ejecting from the bar, they were rapidly banished from inside the place, not outside, so this particular doorman rarely even saw any action anyway. He was there mostly for presence, not purpose. It made for some very lonely and unfulfilling evenings. He felt about as much job satisfaction as a draft excluder.

To combat the monotony of his humdrum position, the doorman would usually stand just inside the doorway and engage the cloakroom attendant in passionate and lively debates. They were almost always about the same thing and almost always ended in the same juvenile way.

"Geez, did you get a good look at them? Cleavage like that is what makes this job worthwhile, if you ask me! I think the one in the white dress might fancy me a bit, actually", the cloakroom attendant volunteered after some scantily-clad ladies had made their way through the doors.
"There's more plastic on them than a box of Tupperware!"
"Yeah, maybe. I wouldn't kick any of 'em out of bed though!"
"Not my type, mate. Girls like that are too stuck up for my tastes, struttin' around with their noses held up so high that they'd probably *drown* in a rainstorm!"
"Come on! You're only saying that 'cause they weren't interested in you! I bet you thought the red head with the big boobs was hot, didn't you? Be honest! I saw you ogling her".
"If by 'hot' you mean that it probably burns when she pees, then yeah! I prefer my women a bit more *natural*, thank you!"
"It's just as well. She probably wouldn't go for a middle-

aged doorman like you anyway".

"Why not? It's better than being a bleedin' cloakroom attendant! My twelve-year-old niece could do *your* job!"

"Yeah? Well *you* could be replaced with a wooden doorstop and a polite notice asking people to behave themselves!"

"Shut up!"

"*You* shut up!"

Like a documentary-maker discreetly observing some strange undiscovered subculture, Lottie listened to the conversation with mild interest and watched with curiosity as the club begin to fill up. She had never been to a place quite like this before. Nobody could see her as she witnessed the excitement from her hidden vantage point, successfully concealed behind a large rack of coats in the kiosk at the club's entrance. The cloakroom vendor didn't mind Lottie hiding there. The monotony of his unfulfilling job had left him with the type of disinterested and non-judgemental personality that would overlook just about anything so long as he was offered a big enough tip. Everybody had a price. His humble price was a double whiskey and coke, it turned out.

"Is there anyone waiting outside yet?" Lottie eventually called out from her hiding place to the doorman, who had rather boldly insisted on two large caffeine drinks and a packet of cigarettes before he would agree to be Lottie's eyes for the evening.

"There's a few more people walking up the street now – a hen party by the looks of things. But your mystery man hasn't shown up yet", he answered to the rack of coats. "Fine. Can you use your security radio to ask someone behind the bar to bring me a lemonade?" the rack of coats politely enquired.
"It'll cost you!"
"It always does".

The DJ switched on his microphone to excitedly announce something completely incomprehensible. Not a single person reacted. He continued to play what Lottie had eventually come to think of as being 'douche music', in that it appeared as though the over-enthused disc jockey was playing the same tuneless song for hours on end, while the repetitive bass boomed: *'douche – douche – douche – clapclap – douche – douche – douche - clapclap'*.

The boisterous hen party eventually staggered its way to the entrance, all of them whooping and cheering loudly at nothing in particular. They paid the entrance fee and coldly ignored the doorman's feeble attempt at flirting with them. The cloakroom attendant made a more conceited effort at earning their favour as he generously dished out free drinks vouchers to all of the women. It was his way of rewarding them for little more than the skimpiness of their crass outfits that struggled to conceal some fairly obvious implants and cosmetic enhancements. Although she would never have admitted it to anyone, Lottie couldn't help but feel a small pang of envy as she witnessed this. What she would have happily admitted to anyone willing to listen, however, was that she also felt somewhat aggrieved by what she considered to be a massively unfair double standard on display. It had always seemed incredibly unjust to her just how often modern society would judge and ridicule someone like herself for a little natural – if unwanted – weight gain, while at the same time celebrating and fawning over women who had arguably put on considerably more weight than Lottie, just because *their* weight expansion happened to come in the form of unnecessary surgeries and unconvincing enhancements. Between all of their artificially swollen lips, cheeks, hips, backsides, boobs and goodness-knows what else, some of these women had probably stuffed more collective synthetic mass into their bodies than Lottie or anyone else could have done with a lifetime of comfort eating and poor diet choices – and yet society seemed to judge Lottie as though *she* was the one who had done something unnatural and weird by allowing herself to become bigger than she once was.

There was a bitter irony to this glaring hypocrisy that didn't escape her attention. She almost began to wonder if it was even worth bothering with her trendy new diet after all, as though it might be a better option to just bypass all the effort and simply pay a surgeon to rearrange her fat into mammoth new breasts and a backside that could fully support a dinner plate.

She snapped out of this sulky observation as soon as the gaggle of silicon women made their way to the bar, and she realised that the doorman was talking about the same women to the cloakroom attendant.

"...And I'm telling *you*, it doesn't matter how good, how big or convincing they look. You just can't beat the *real* thing!"

Lottie smiled smugly from behind the coats. At least the doorman seemed to agree with her point of view!

"Women like that are basically just sacks of silicon and scar tissue. I always prefer skinny girls myself. They seem to dress nicer anyway", he went on. He then turned to face the rack of coats and loudly added, "No offense to you in there, love", which instantly caused Lottie enormous offense.

"I'll have you know…" Lottie indignantly raged from her hiding place, "… that I may have temporarily gained a little weight recently, but I'm *perfectly happy* with my natural curves, thank you very much! And not that it's any of your business either way but these clothes are in fact very expensive designer garments, and I'm actually on a new diet now anyway so I plan on giving them all to a charity for people who are starving and homeless very soon. So, that shows how much *you* know!"

"What I *do* know…" the bemused bouncer cockily fired

back, "...is that your photographer friend has just got out of a car outside with another man. Oh, and I wouldn't waste your time donating those clothes, love. Anyone who can fit into *your* clothes clearly isn't starving!"

Before Lottie could think of a witty and scathing response to this, her debate with the doorman came to an abrupt end as a very curiously dressed young man entered the club. He appeared to be wearing a small wig, a pair of sunglasses, an oversized coat and a large red baseball cap – a ridiculous disguise that actually made him look as inconspicuous as a pink elephant boarding a bus while shooting fireworks out of its trunk. He walked through the main door into the lobby area, and before the bouncer could question anything, the man discreetly placed two crisp fifty-pound notes into his hand and told him, "You don't recognise me and you didn't see any of this".

The strange man then proceeded to remove his outlandish disguise, placed the items into a small designer bag that was slung across his broad shoulder, and intriguingly he then turned and walked straight outside again. This time, his handsome chiselled face was fully exposed to the photographer, who was now taking pictures of the mysterious man leaving the club from across the street. As the peculiar man jumped into a waiting taxi and quickly disappeared into the night, Lottie haughtily pushed her way past the doorman, exited the club and tried not to look directly at the cameraman who was still positioned on the other side of the street. She held her head down and covered her eyes deliberately so as to give the impression that she was trying hard *not* to be noticed. Unfortunately, she tried a bit too hard and achieved this too effectively, so the paparazzi photographer had to order her back inside the nightclub so that she could stage her photos for a second time.

"What the hell was all that about?" the bewildered cloakroom attendant asked the doorman after Lottie, the mysterious man and the photographer had all finally gone their separate ways.

"I don't know. I guess someone really wanted to be seen leaving this club. I can't imagine why anyone'd want to photographed leaving *here*, though".

"That man with the wig… he looked familiar. That was *Roger Scott*, wasn't it? The ex-footballer who's been in all the papers lately?"

The doorman thought about the hundred pounds in his pocket and remembered that the other chap hadn't actually seen him accept the small bribe. "I don't think so", he lied, "But I think that the fat girl might have been the one who was on *Women's Natter* a few weeks ago, when that bonkers Mrs O got suspended. Have you seen the video clip yet?"

....

It was another late night in the *Celebs Today* offices for David. He was sitting in solitude, and the stillness and silence of the unoccupied office building weighed heavily as it enclosed him. The fuzzy light from his computer screen and a small ineffective desktop lamp provided the only break from complete darkness as David half-heartedly skimmed through another costly letter from his expensive divorce lawyer. It explained how David's estranged wife was now seeking an official 'Safeguard Order for Exclusive Use of the Family Residence' ruling and as a bonus, she was also threatening to request a restraining order too. What this essentially meant was that Angelica was taking a legal route to ask that David be prohibited from returning to the marital home, and she was also asking for legal permission to change the locks. The reason for this, according to the letter, was Angelica's claim that their last physical interaction – during which David had tried his best to calmly reason with her and she had dropped a full bucket of ice cold water on his head – had left her terrified for her own safety. Not so terrified that she would consider leaving and finding her own place to live, it seemed, but apparently terrified enough that she wanted to ban David from coming anywhere near his own home. Predictably, whatever trauma she had experienced as a result of turning David away a few weeks earlier could easily be cured with a generous financial compensation, at least according to her recent counter offer of a divorce settlement.

David scoffed aloud as he turned the page and read that

the potential restraining order she was threatening to seek would also specifically name their *dog* as well. She was quite literally threatening to try and legally ban David from coming within a certain distance of his own dog, unless of course, they could *'reach an amicable agreement that would satisfy both parties in the meantime'*.

It was thinly disguised extortion at best. It began to occur to David, not for the first time, that Angelica didn't even really *want* some of the items she was asking for in the divorce. Except for the money, which always was and always would be her one true love after herself. But some of the other effects they were disputing about in the break up came down to pure malicious pettiness; she didn't even like to drive the expensive car she was requesting, she hadn't ever shown any personal attachment to the specific furnishings that they were fighting over and she had never particularly liked the dog very much at all. It seemed to David that Angelica simply didn't want *him* to have those things.

It was about control, power and capricious nastiness. She appeared to be playing a very shrewd and spiteful game of taking away things that she knew David loved and would miss. She wanted to take what he wanted to have, purely out of spite.
But the one thing that David now wanted more than anything else in the world was to do the same to her.
It was fast becoming a dangerous game to play.

Chapter Thirteen

"So, they just *happened* to be seen leaving the same random backstreet nightclub together at the same time? And we're expected to believe this was just a coincidence and that they weren't secretly partying together?" Cherlene jealously raged at her unlucky new agent, who obediently nodded in agreement and tried his best to look interested. "And look, in *this* photo *she* is leaving his house, and if you look at *this* newspaper you can see that they were in the same restaurant together a few weeks ago too. They've obviously been trying to hide it but they're *clearly* in a relationship! Not that *I* care, obviously".

Cherlene was sat with her new talent agent, Teddy. She had chosen to hire Teddy as her public representative to replace PR guru Clive Maxwell, who had recently taken the unusual principled step of deciding that he could no longer fairly represent Cherlene *and* the man she was divorcing at the same time.

Although he had claimed that ethical integrity was the reason he had formally broken ties with her, Cherlene quite accurately suspected that Clive Maxwell had in fact felt aggrieved by her recent underhanded behaviour in the handling of the marital separation. Clive had decided that his distinguished and much sought-after loyalties should remain firmly with Roger Scott instead of the wife who was trying to undermine him, and so he had decided to stop representing her professionally. Teddy, by contrast, had always been a stranger to alien concepts like *ethics* or *loyalty*, and was perfectly happy to add just about any celebrity leftovers to his questionable client list. This was a far more typical approach adopted by the unscrupulous entertainment industry to these types of ethical conundrums.

Today was Teddy and Cherlene's first formal meeting together as agent and client, but rather than discussing how best to capitalise on Cherlene's newly acquired potential as a household name as Teddy had originally intended, he reluctantly found himself engaged in a one-sided discussion about Roger and Lottie's sizzling new relationship. Cherlene was doing almost one hundred percent of the talking.

"I *knew* something was suspicious as soon as she denied on TwitchFace that she had been seeing him. I could tell that was a lie! Then when they were seen sneaking out of that cheap club together and blatantly trying to hide from the paps, my suspicions were confirmed! I knew they wouldn't do that unless they *really* had something to hide", Cherlene continued to fume, completely unprompted and entirely unaware that - like the rest of the country - she was falling for a lie. She had arrived at Teddy's office brandishing dozens of recent tabloids that had published reports of Roger and Lottie's rumoured new romance, and for no obvious reason she seemed determined to fully explore each of them with obsessive scrutiny.

"Not that *I'm* bothered, of course! Don't think I'm bothered by this, 'cause I'm not!" she rambled unconvincingly. "We'll be formally divorced soon anyway, so he can date whoever he wants. It's none of *my* concern if he chooses to date some washed up reality TV star who, by the way, is nowhere near as pretty as me on her best day!"

"I think she looks okay, personally", Teddy grumbled quietly. Although he had recently lost Lottie as a client and still didn't know the real reason why, he hadn't taken her decision personally and felt somewhat that he ought to at least try and defend her in her absence.

"*Jealous*? I'm not jealous!" Cherlene inexplicably raged, even though nobody had actually suggested that she was. Teddy was clearly not an active or even necessary part of this conversation as far as Cherlene was concerned. He wondered if he could sneak out for a quick bite to eat without her noticing. "I just happen to think that she looks like ten pounds of garbage stuffed into a five-pound sack, but that's just my opinion. Not that I care", she continued to gripe, entirely unabated.

"Yes, yes. Well now that's settled, let's get back to business, shall we? I've got a couple of potential auditions for you that we can discuss, and also a –"
"And did you see the pictures of them lumbering around

on the beach together? She's crammed into that swimsuit like a badly packed sausage, and he's grinning like a love-struck teenager! All I'm saying is that he never used to look like he was going to give himself a hernia whenever he carried *me* across the sand like that. She's got a beach body like a beer barrel compared to *me!*"

"Well, moving on –"

"Not that *I* care, anyway…"

"Well, *moving on*, I still wanted to discuss –"

"And you say that they've actually done a cheesy magazine feature interview together?"

Teddy finally gave up. He had hoped that today would be a productive meeting full of creative discussions and lucrative ideas with his profitable new client. Unfortunately, it was now becoming painstakingly clear that Cherlene was fighting a losing battle with jealousy over her ex-husband's new relationship, despite her persistently gallant efforts to deny it.

He sighed. "Yes, that's what I've heard. In next week's *Celebs Today*, Lottie and Roger are going to formally confirm their relationship and tell their story. They've done their interview already, apparently, and it's being pieced together ready for publication as we speak". Teddy paused for a moment. He suddenly had the vague recollection of sending Lottie to the *Celebs Today* office a few weeks prior to meet with an editor that he once knew. The words "executive editor", "PR stunt" and "sham romance" came teasingly close to reaching the surface of his conscious mind, but ultimately not close enough. He quickly dismissed the fleeting thought. It was probably just a coincidence.

"It says *here* that the story was written by Walter Plinge. Do you know who that is?" Cherlene asked accusingly, as she pointed to a recent article about her ex in *Celebs Today*.

"That sounds like a pseudonym to me. You know, when somebody publishes something but doesn't want their real name attached to it, for whatever reason", Teddy replied. "Speaking of which, what is *your* name now? I noticed that you signed your name as 'To Be Decided' on some forms earlier, and I don't actually know what your maiden name is. Are you going to keep calling yourself Cherlene Scott after the divorce?"

"Yes, why not? Actually… no. Well, maybe. I haven't really decided yet, to be honest. I don't really want to go back to my maiden name. Cherlene *Fleecey* just doesn't quite have the same ring to it. It makes me sound like I'm either made of tweed or that I'm some kind of chancer who's about to fleece somebody".
Teddy agreed sympathetically. "You could try using a mononym", he tactically suggested.

Cherlene's pained expression turned blank and remained fixed for a moment. Unfortunately, Teddy would never know whether this was because she either hadn't liked or simply hadn't understood his suggestion of using a mononym professionally, because there was clearly only room for one topic to occupy her mind today.

"I'm actually *happy* Roger has moved on!" she erratically blurted out, magnetically returning to the theme of her ex as if answering a question that nobody had even asked. "I'm *perfectly* happy being single, and I wish him well with his new chubby girlfriend".

Before Teddy could even attempt to change the subject yet again, Cherlene - purely out of a mild curiosity that clearly had nothing at all to do with the ex-husband she definitely wasn't jealous of – meekly asked, "Do you, um, happen to get a lot of single men in these offices? Models, um, footballers or whatever?"

....

The following week, *Celebs Today* hit the newsstands as normal. Just below the main cover story was the tantalising headline: *"Roger Scott & Lottie Klünt Exclusively Reveal All"*. Although they weren't the main story in the issue, David had assured them that their engagement announcement and eventual breakup would certainly make all of the main headlines. It was only a matter of time.

Inside the magazine was an exclusive interview that spread over four pages, and featured a rather nauseating glossy photo shoot of the couple gazing lovingly into one another's eyes, wearing cheesy matching outfits and lying together on a bed of white feathers. Nobody had ever been able to successfully explain why these magazines so often opted to stage such naff images when photographing couples together, but stomach-churning photos seemed to be the industry standard when illustrating any kind of romance for its readership.

However banal the photo shoot might have been, the corny pictures fully served their cynical purpose. Lottie and Roger had finally announced to the world that they were definitely in a relationship, completely in love and totally committed to a future together. If all continued to go to plan, only Lottie, Roger and David would ever know that none of this was even remotely true.

As with Cherlene's interview a few months prior, David Paige had personally helped to craft the exclusive tell-all confirmation of the new romance. He had drafted all of the questions, written the magazine's narrative of meeting the couple face to face and had even dictated most of Lottie and Roger's answers, which he had insisted they read into a tape recorder, purely on the off chance that anybody one day questioned the authenticity of it.

Steered by David, Lottie had used the interview to dismiss concerns that her relationship with a known serial adulterer was doomed from the start: "*He's learned from his past mistakes. Besides, if he ever cheated on me, I would kill him! I'm not worried about that – but he should be!*" she had playfully answered to a question about fidelity.

Roger – guided equally by David - had taken the opportunity to publicly declare his love for Lottie and to dismiss inevitable criticism that he was moving on from his failed marriage too quickly: "*We're in love and it's real. When you get a second chance at love, you don't hesitate; you take it and embrace it!*"

They had even revealed their sickeningly sweet pet names for one another, which was another little detail dreamt up by David to make them seem more genuine: "*I call her Lottie Love, 'cause she gives me a 'lot-of-love', and she calls me Mr Scotty*".

The magazine issue sold well. Other publications began to report on the surprising new romance – totally unaware that it was all a con - and like a fame-addict who had been offered another hit, Lottie finally began to feel that she was receiving positive attention again.

What the public didn't know was that Lottie and Roger had secretly given *two* different interviews to *Celebs Today* on that day. The first one was to confirm their relationship, which had now been published, but the second one was to confirm their *engagement*; David was already planning to publish the second one in just a few weeks' time!

The lies were piling up thick and fast, and everything was going exactly according to the plan.

....

Lottie looked at herself in the mirror while the makeup artist's apprentice/daughter worked her magic. Except for the occasional stab in the eye with an eyeliner pencil from the well-meaning but blatantly inexperienced makeup girl, Lottie was beginning to feel a little better about her appearance already. After dieting for just four weeks she had proudly lost almost *four* whole pounds, and had already somewhat prematurely treated herself to an entire new glamorous wardrobe to suit her slightly slimmer frame. She had even promised to reward herself with another indulgent shopping spree of even more expensive new clothes if she could lose as much as six pounds by Christmas. It was relatively easy, if you didn't count the perpetual hunger.

"Are you almost ready in there? We need you live on the air in fifteen minutes, Lottie", assistant show director Pete Waters asked tentatively as he peered around the door into the makeup room.

"Yes I think we're almost done here. I'm looking forward to – *ouch*!"
"Sorry about that! My finger slipped. Let me just wipe your eye for you. Oh no, that's just smudged it again... Let me just – oops!"
"I think we'll just need a couple of minutes more".

Pete smiled and left. The makeup artist set to work again frantically trying to repair whatever damage she had just clumsily inflicted, and Lottie continued to look at her reflection in the mirror with her one good eye. She felt fairly nervous but tried her best to remain calm and keep positive. Things were going well, she told herself, and things were about to become even better.

Lottie's fake relationship with Roger Scott was already providing her with the precious press attention she had hoped for, especially coming so close after his much-discussed marriage breakdown, and she couldn't have been any happier about it. People gradually seemed to be forgetting about Lottie's humiliating incident with

Mrs O a few months ago, and she was trying to embrace the new attention to portray herself in a more positive light again. Quite understandably, David and Roger only seemed to be looking forward to the *next* part – the staged public showdown, Lottie's broken heart and Roger's stint in rehab – but for Lottie, she could already feel the upswing of the celebrity publicity pendulum beginning to work in her favour once again.

Photo agencies were suddenly receiving more requests for, and found themselves able to charge more money for, paparazzi photos of Lottie. She wasn't exactly being bombarded like Britney Spears, but she was at least able to take advantage of the public's mild interest in her better than she had at any point in the last two years. She even began receiving party invitations and social media interactions from other minor celebrities, which was always a good sign. In Lottie's experience, celebrity friends were like shadows; they were permanently by your side when you were under the spotlight but they immediately disappeared in the darkness. This was just the beginning. *"By the time this is all over, you'll be the most famous woman in Britain"*, David had promised her, and these words reassuringly repeated in Lottie's mind over and over anytime that she had doubts about the cynical plan.

"Okay, I think I'm all finished here!" the junior makeup artist announced, smiling proudly at her handiwork. "Just try not to turn your head to the left too much, don't

171

move *this* strand of hair and make sure you don't touch your face at all. Good luck!"

As the woman called Pete Waters back to escort Lottie to the television studio set, Lottie's phone began to ring. She saw that the call was coming from an unrecognised landline number and knew straight away who would be on the other end of the line. David appeared to be going to extraordinary lengths to cover his tracks when speaking to her, and it occurred to Lottie that he must have spent ages trawling for some of Britain's few remaining public phone boxes from which to call her.

She answered. As expected, it was David.

"It's you-know-who. I'm just calling to let you know that Roger and Cherlene's marriage has now been formally dissolved. It's all official. They were awarded their decree absolute this morning, so we're going to wait a week for that news to die down and then we'll go ahead and publish your engagement announcement. Be *careful*, tell *no-one* and get *ready* – you're going to be the most famous woman in Britain when this is all over!"

Lottie agreed and hung up the phone. She could feel a sense of anticipation and giddiness, and was barely able to stifle her grin as she was led to the set and sat down once again on mid-morning television's most iconic sofa. This was almost how being famous had felt in the very beginning. It was an utterly addictive sensation.

"Dinnae worry 'bout last time you were on the show, love", the temporary host replacement of Mrs O reassured Lottie in a thick Scottish accent while the director hushed the studio audience into silence. "No-one'll remember yer wee outburst from before, and I've been practisin' how to say yer name properly all mornin', just in case".

"Okay ladies… we are broadcasting live in three, two, one…"
The audience applauded.

"Good morning! Welcome to *Women's Natter*!" the provisional presenter enthusiastically announced, her distinctive Glaswegian drawl suddenly disappearing faster than a toupee in a hurricane, "On today's programme, it's our special time of the month when we have Chef Richards showing us the creamiest desserts that can be prepared in under twenty minutes. Also, we have psychologist Maxine Paddy discussing how women are harming ourselves by focussing too much on body image, and Doctor Tammy Mason is going to teach us simple diet tips for women who want to lose those extra pounds without hitting the gym! But first, we have reality TV star Lottie - K-l-o-o-n-t - joining us on the sofa as she discusses her controversial new romance with Roger Scott, her bid for privacy after all the recent press intrusion and denies new pregnancy rumours after *those* unflattering swimsuit pictures were taken at the local pool".

Chapter Fourteen

'Learning to drive is perhaps the most liberating thing you will ever learn...' Lottie remembered her Dad once telling her as a child.

'All you need in life is a full tank of fuel in your car and your favourite songs on the stereo...' another pearl of her father's wisdom came to mind.

'We may not always feel equal in life, but with a steering wheel in your hands and an open road in front of you, every man and woman feels equal in their own destiny...' a separate childhood memory resurfaced itself.

"My Dad really did talk a lot of bollocks!" Lottie suddenly huffed aloud, snapping irritably back into reality.

She had been sitting alone in slow moving motorway traffic for one extremely long and uncomfortable hour, and she was becoming increasingly annoyed by it all. Her determined efforts at achieving a calm, Zen-like mindset of serene thoughts and patience were no match for the M1 on a bad day, and her tolerance had almost completely run out fifty-six minutes earlier. Although she had always liked that her parents were out there living their lives in a quiet little village far away from Lottie's home in London – mainly because it meant that they couldn't visit very often – she also hated that 'far away' was such a pain in the proverbial to drive to. The traffic suddenly came to a complete stop again. In spite of this, every car surrounding her seemed to be impatiently creeping forward as much as was physically possible until the cars were practically touching bumper-to-bumper, as though the other road users were hoping against the odds to somehow defeat the traffic standstill inch by inch. A couple of drivers announced their impatience by sounding their horns aggressively. Lottie turned around to glare at them with a deeply sarcastic expression of open-mouthed mock surprise that even *this* act of brilliance didn't make the traffic jam suddenly disappear into nonexistence.

She turned on the car radio again. Annoyingly, a broken button on the touchscreen had rendered the stereo hopelessly stuck on the same lousy pop radio station for several weeks now. To Lottie's complete lack of surprise, the obnoxious hosts were still chatting inanely over the same half a dozen songs they had been playing all day, just like they did every other day. Lottie hit the 'off' button with an irritable whack, muttered a few unladylike words about the insufferable hosts that would have horrified her mother, and finally accepted that she was going to have to face the unwelcome task of calling her parents today after all. She knew that they were not going to be at all pleased with her today and had hoped to at least break the bad news to them in person before they read it in the press; Lottie and Roger's engagement had been publicly announced that very morning, and owing to a slight mix up on Lottie's part about the actual date, she hadn't had a chance to inform her parents anything about it beforehand.

She switched on the hands-free device and apprehensively dialled the phone number. Maybe she would be lucky, she tried in vain to reassure herself. Maybe her parents hadn't read any of the tabloids yet.

"Hello?"
"Hello, Daddy? It's me".
"Lottie! *Finally*! The famous bride-to-be! You grace us with a telephone call! What an *honour*! I was almost beginning to wonder if you remembered that you even *have* parents!"

'*Bollocks! Bollocks! Bollocks!*' Lottie cursed noiselessly under her breath. She had obviously left it too late. This was bad.

"Daddy, I was coming to tell you the news in person but I'm stuck in really bad traffic. A lorry has spilled its load all over the – "

"Of course, a *visit* would have been nice! But I suppose that's too much to ask from our *only daughter*, isn't it? I suppose I'm just being old fashioned, but I didn't expect to learn the news that my *only daughter* is getting married from the local bloody newsagent!"

"Daddy, I'm really sorry. I just got my weeks mixed up, and I thought – "

"I suppose you were too busy gallivanting with all your fancy celebrity friends and new fiancé to bother thinking about how your boring old parents might feel, not knowing anything about their *only daughter's* engagement! Just wait until your poor mother hears about this!"

"She's... um... She's not there, then?" Lottie asked cautiously, desperately trying to disguise any trace or hint of relief from her voice. Her Dad might whinge and occasionally employ the odd guilt trip when he was upset, but that was nothing compared to Lottie's mother. The woman was in a league of her own when it came to emotional manipulation. She could make you feel genuine remorse for behaviour you were accused of in a previous lifetime. She could make people honour a promise in real life that they had only made to her in a dream. If she hit you with her car, you would probably end up cleaning her bonnet for her and sending her a note of apology for the inconvenience.

"No, she's in Antwerp taking care of her *Bibles-For-A-More-Biblical-Belgium-Within-Borders* campaign in schools. Apparently, they've run into some difficulties as most of the schools don't want them, and there's some minor technical issue about it being a secular country that separates church and state or something. They've threatened to arrest her if she doesn't stop, but you know what your mother's like! Anyway, I assume she doesn't know the news about you yet. I spoke to her last night, and she just said that she'll be praying to God for you".

"Right, thanks. Tell her I'll be writing to Father Christmas for her!" Lottie's sullen response automatically rolled off her tongue before she could stop the words from escaping. Today was not the day for sarcasm, she reminded herself.

"Today is *not* the day for sarcasm, young lady!" her father uncannily snapped back. "You know that your mother never approved of you running off to London to be some big television star in the first place. She was devastated when you stopped using the family Van de Klünt name. Just imagine how upset she'll be now when she hears that you're going to become *Mrs Lottie Scotty!*"

Lottie rolled her eyes. She had known that she would come to regret the stupid 'Mr Scotty' nickname David had written in the interview from the very moment he had suggested it. Her Dad went on, "Honestly, aside from everything else... why Roger bloody Scott? Is it a self-esteem thing? The ink's barely even dry on his divorce papers, and yet you're already rushing down the aisle after nothing more than a quick fling! I had higher hopes for my *only daughter* than marrying some gormless ex footballer who can't keep his unmentionables in his pants for more than five minutes. I suppose he's probably very impressive with his good looks, flashy cars and so on, but that stuff never lasts! He's hardly the sharpest tool in the shed, is he? He's just a stupid, buggery... tool! And that makes *you* a very naïve... Well, it makes you a very short-sighted... Well, that just makes you a shed!"

Lottie winced at both her Dad's clumsy crude analogy and his very reasonable argument. How could she ever explain this one? Even if – hypothetically - her engagement to Roger wasn't all a big sham and she did really want to marry the man, her Dad brought up several good points that Lottie couldn't realistically dispute with genuine conviction. She had to choose her words very carefully lest she draw too much suspicion to herself. She opened her mouth to speak, but then quickly paused again. Suddenly, she began to wonder if she ought to just let her Dad know the truth about the entire charade after all.

"You can't judge him by what you read in the press, Daddy! They only write about the superficial stuff and the gossip. They don't know what's inside him", she insisted as convincingly as she could. She was still having second thoughts about committing to such a big lie even to her parents, and was internally trying to decide if it was really worth keeping up the pretence, or if she should just give up and explain the whole truth to her Dad right now.

"Lottie, the man is a moron and a womaniser. Don't try and convince me that there's some profoundly misunderstood deep thinker inside him, because I just won't believe it. He probably wouldn't know if there was a bloody *train* inside him unless somebody blew the whistle!" her Dad fired back, quite accurately.

David had been quite insistent from the very beginning that nobody – *nobody at all* – should know what he, Roger and Lottie were planning. He had even told them that he wasn't going to tell his boss at *Celebs Today* that he was actively helping to craft the sham romance. He had repeatedly hammered home the point that if anybody even suspected that Lottie and Roger had staged their entire romance and breakup, they would risk exposing themselves to a humiliation that would irredeemably destroy all their careers and reputations. It would be infinitely worse than any scandal or PR disaster they had ever experienced. They would never be able to show their faces in public again. It simply wasn't worth the risk.

Even now, Lottie was already beginning to have further second thoughts about her first second thoughts. The more she thought about it, the more it made sense again that she should keep her parents unaware after all. They wouldn't feel any better about the situation to know that it was all just a sham romance leading to an orchestrated breakup just for publicity in any case. They would be no less upset and judgemental to know that their only daughter was taking part in such a contrived PR stunt as they would be to think that Lottie had become engaged during some ill-advised whirlwind romance. They could never truly understand why she felt she needed to do this anyway. How could they possibly? They would never know what it actually *felt* like to be famous, to experience the incomparable sense of validation that came with being adored on such a large scale, to be able to see themselves through the eyes of the whole country, and then to suddenly feel that fame beginning to slip away from them through their fingers faster than quicksand. They would never know the torment of being thought of as nothing more than a *'has-been'* forevermore, as though the only meaningful part of their lives was a flash in the pan that had already been and gone in less than half a decade, and would likely never ever come back. For Lottie, it was barely even about chasing the spotlight anymore. It was more about trying to escape the dreaded black void of obscurity that every celebrity, big or small, knew was perpetually looming just *beyond* the spotlight. After all these years and all the effort that she had put into building and establishing her public persona, and living her life through the glare of the media, she would be damned if she would end up only remembered for being nothing more than a girl whose name was accidentally mispronounced as a vulgar profanity on a daytime television show.

No, Lottie decided, it was probably better to let them think it was a real romance for now. At least that way, they were spared the pressure of keeping her big secret, Lottie was spared a lot of heavy lectures from her parents, and nobody had to worry about them potentially leaking any information that might ruin the plan.
It would all be over in a few weeks' time anyway, she reassured herself, so why rock the boat now?

"He's a good man, Daddy", she sighed after a moment. "I know what I'm doing, and that's all I can tell you right now. I'm afraid you'll just have to trust me on this".

....

David said nothing. He wordlessly slid the photos, carefully concealed in a plain brown envelope, across the table to the man who had given them to him.

"And you're certain about this?" David wearily asked after a long and heavy silence. "It's important that you're absolutely certain. There's no chance you've made some kind of mistake?"

"I don't make guesses in my profession", the private detective responded, maintaining a calm monotone that expertly hid his minor annoyance at the offensive suggestion. "I just investigate what I'm asked to investigate, provide you with all the photos and the evidence that I find, and then it's entirely up to you to interpret it all".

David was stunned. Even after all these years, Angelica could still surprise him.
"Ashton Cain, of all people? What could she possibly see in *him*?"

The detective paused uncertainly for a moment. Despite what people might think about his profession, he took absolutely no personal interest in his clients' private lives or the activities he was being paid to investigate. He was asked to find facts, he found facts and he delivered facts. He didn't speculate. He wasn't curious. He didn't give opinions. He certainly never involved himself. However, surely even a client like David could imagine why his estranged wife might suddenly be interested in dating a much younger, much more handsome man than the middle-aged husband she was in the process of divorcing.

"It's not for me to speculate", he tactically responded. "I was only supposed to be following Mrs Paige, but I did find out along the way that Mr Cain has been approaching some modelling agencies. Despite his relatively young age, he's currently the top editor in charge of a tabloid magazine called *Celebs Today* and it seems like he earns very good money, but there's one modelling agency in particular that he keeps going back to, so I would hazard a cautious guess that he might have signed a contract with them and might be looking for a career change. Maybe he wants to try *being* a glamorous famous model instead of just writing about them. I guess his job has given him a lot of valuable connections in the 'biz, and I suppose it's not so incomprehensible that a recently single woman might have her attentions attracted by a handsome model type. Want me to keep an eye on him too?"

"No", David responded flatly. This was certainly an unexpected development, but it was important to him to keep to the original plan, for now at least. He mustn't become distracted this late in the game. "So, the other man?"

"Again, I don't like to speculate. I just show you the photos of what I've seen. As far as I can tell, he and Angelica are not seeing each other anymore. But she does keep driving by his house for no obvious purpose and it seems as though she's keeping tabs on him. As far as I know, he's just become engaged to someone else anyway. Perhaps you already knew this?"

Again, David said nothing.

"Look, on a personal level, I wouldn't worry too much about Ashton Cain. I don't speculate professionally, but it seems to me that she's still very much infatuated with the other guy. A lesser professional might even suggest that she's just trying to make him jealous by dating Mr Cain. But, as you know, I only deal in facts".

....

Lottie was surprised to see that Roger was already waiting in the restaurant's large empty kitchen as the manager directed her inside through the back door. She had actually arrived on time, which was basically tantamount to being incredibly early by her unique standards, and she had therefore expected to be the first one there. The restaurant manager invited Lottie to help herself to the snacks that had been thoughtfully laid out for the two of them, and then left them alone. The restaurant technically wouldn't open to the public for another four hours, but he had made an exception for Lottie and Roger when somebody had called him – presumably a representative of theirs – to explain how the famous newly betrothed couple were looking for an idyllic location for a romantic lunch that was viewable from the street. It didn't take a genius to work out that they were more interested in a public photo opportunity than the upmarket restaurant's fine dining, but the manager had received a modest under-the-table fee for allowing this exception that he didn't need to declare to his head office, and the publicity generated today certainly wouldn't do the business any harm.
Roger and Lottie greeted each other awkwardly. They

smiled politely, exchanged a couple of mild pleasantries about the weather and location... and then completely ran out of things to say to one another. It was finally beginning to occur to them both that even though they had technically become 'engaged' the week before, this was actually the first time they had had to spend any significant time alone with one another. Not only that, but once they were eventually seated at the table outside and all the paparazzi photographers arrived to take pictures of them, Lottie and Roger would be staging what was technically their very first kiss too. And once they had done it, nobody but them would know that this was the first time they had actually kissed each other. Up until now, David had been relatively concerned about the couple overselling and overexposing themselves too soon before the main event, which was to be the pre-planned drama of their explosive breakup. He had been very cautious and astute in his planning and orchestrating of the sham romance, carefully trying to enthral the public's interest in Lottie and Roger as a celebrity couple without exhausting the hype too quickly and inadvertently causing people to lose interest too soon. David was expertly exploiting what was a very delicate fine line in public relations that a lot of celebrities had navigated so poorly in the past.

With the exception of the two *Celebs Today* interviews confirming their relationship and subsequent engagement, Lottie and Roger's entire romance had so far been largely portrayed through the strategic pretence of trying to keep it low key and secretive; paparazzi would 'catch' them leaving each other's houses, discreetly exiting the same venue or playfully enjoying one another's company on what had been staged to look like a romantic beach trip. Great care was being executed to make it seem as though they were trying *not* to draw attention to themselves, when in reality drawing attention to themselves was the entire point of the relationship. With every passing week, David had been gradually drip-feeding more and more images of the couple together through the media. Today, he wanted to see close up paparazzi photographs of the happy couple kissing over a romantic lunch. They would make a great contrast to the images that would be published next weekend when the fake couple finally staged their explosive breakup.

"These mini hamburgers are good", Roger announced, kindly offering Lottie one of the many plates of food that had been left out for them. "You're not a vegetarian or anything like that, are you?"

"Not at all", Lottie responded, already deciding that today would be another 'cheat day' from her strict new diet. She had always been something of a nervous eater. She was also very much a comfort eater and usually a bit of an emotional eater. She had a tendency to eat quite a lot when she was a bit bored, too. "I'll just take three of these and a couple of these croquettes. And maybe a few of these little cakes. I don't want to fill myself up too much 'cause we'll be having lunch soon. Do you know what time the paps will be arriving?"

"I've got no idea", Roger answered. "I just let David sort all that stuff out. He's been a really great guy with all the help he's been giving us, don't you think?"

Lottie gave a half shrug of acknowledgement as she helped herself to another handful of mini hamburgers. They really *were* good. Roger broke into a relaxed smile. A new thought suddenly entered his head and – as was customary for Roger whenever this occurred – he immediately decided to verbalise it.
"You know what? Cherlene, my ex-wife, she never used to eat in public. She hated a lot of silly things like that. In fact, she would barely even eat in private. All she cared about was how she looked. She used to say, '*I want my belt to still buckle when I'm finished eating, not my chair!*', although if I'm being honest I never fully understood what that meant. All she cared about was being thin and pretty. You seem very different though".

Lottie's jaw dropped at Roger's brutally honest observation, or at least it attempted to. The two mini hamburgers she had shoved into her mouth moments before rather spoiled the indignant effect. Roger continued his thought unremittingly, "You seem a lot more fun. I like it".

Lottie decided to simply accept what was now clearly meant as a compliment without asking any more questions. Roger's childlike honesty could be horribly offensive or rather sweet, depending on how you chose to view it. She sometimes wondered how other people took to him.

"So, how long were you and Cherlene married for?" Lottie asked. She wasn't particularly interested and had asked the question mainly for the sake of having something to say. It was beginning to dawn on her that David obviously hadn't expected her to actually turn up on time today and had probably very slyly arranged for the paparazzi to turn up at a much later time than he had agreed with her. This often happened. Even TV producers used to tell Lottie to turn up at four o'clock when they had told everyone to arrive at five o'clock, so that they would all more or less arrive at the same time. Lottie could have been quite cross at this but for the irritating fact that she still fell for it almost every time.

"We were married for about four years, I think", Roger answered, with complete inaccuracy that didn't surprise Lottie for a moment. Even she could remember that the Scott's lavish public spectacle of a wedding reception was at least six years ago. "But I don't think we'll ever get back together", Roger went on. "In fact, I'm not even seeing anyone at all right now. My agent Clive told me that I need to calm down and give myself a break from little flings for a while, you know, after the divorce and the scandals with women. He's probably right. How about you? Do you have a... I mean, are you, um, sort of, y'know... sexually active right now?"

"Not exactly", Lottie shrugged, with a look that suggested that this situation was not by choice. "Frankly, I'm barely even *socially* active right now! Perhaps when this is all over, I'll start looking for something a little more... real. Maybe I'll settle down with someone nice."

"It's funny", Roger smiled, "But for me, this is probably the most monogamous relationship I've ever had, and we both already know that next week you're gonna break up with me for cheating on you!"

Lottie laughed. This was the first time she had heard Roger make a joke. It was also the first time she had even heard him use a word as big as 'monogamous' without becoming hopelessly tongue-tied and confused. She opened the door through to the restaurant and risked a glance outside. The restaurant manager was sitting alone by the window. He knew exactly what she was looking for. "No photographers are outside yet. Don't worry, I'll come get you as soon as they arrive", he informed Lottie without even looking up from the newspaper he was reading. She impatiently stomped back into the kitchen. She also secretly made a solemn

191

vow to herself that she would never be on time anywhere ever again. It wasn't worth it. She had never considered patience to be a virtue.

"So how about you?" she asked Roger, now deciding that she was definitely bored. "What'll you do when this is all over with? I know that the plan is for you to check into rehab for sex addiction and then come out like some kind of *born again* champion who's conquered his demons and so on, but what about after *that*? Will you return to professional football perhaps?"

"It is probably a bit late for all that", Roger responded sadly. "It's not like being an actor or a singer or a… whatever you are. You've only got a short time when you're at your peak as a footballer. I'll probably never get back to my glory days or be taken that seriously again. I'd just never expected it all to be over so soon".

"So… why not give up on the whole fame thing then? I don't mean to be rude, I'm just curious as to why you care enough to go through all this effort. What's the point if there's no end goal, so to speak?"

"Money! That's it, frankly. I've wasted quite a lot of my fortune already. I was earning so much money at one point and I was probably too young to know what to do with it. I kind of thought it was endless. Bit silly really. They never really warn you about that stuff when you're at the top of your game. Then I spent a few weeks in prison for that drink driving business, which, with hindsight, I probably regret now if I'm being perfectly honest. That cost me a lot. I came out of prison with no money and no job, and stupidly I fell for the temptation of having an affair... Well, um, quite a lot of times actually. So, that cost me my marriage and that cost me even more money! My agent reckons I can still be famous enough to get rich again just from sponsorship deals and stuff, but only if I can change my image first... so that's where you come in. I kind of wish I could just go back to playing football instead, but you know how it is".

"It sounds like you really miss it. Maybe you could teach? Be a football coach to kids and, y'know, find the next big star or something?"

"I don't think anyone'd want me teaching their kids. People kind of hate me right now. Besides, most of the kids would probably be smarter than me anyway! I'm not exactly the brightest bean in the bucket. I probably wouldn't be very good".

"But..." Lottie sought for the right words. Although she hadn't spent much time in Roger's company before, she had certainly never expected him to be like this. It was almost disconcerting the way that Roger – a man she had hitherto considered to have the emotional and overall intelligence of a Beanie Baby – was suddenly speaking in such a wistful and self-deprecating manner. Guiltily, she began to realise that up until now she had been completely judging the man by his dubious public persona. "I guess being knocked off your pedestal changes the way you think about things", she said at last, thoughtfully. "Maybe by the time this is all over, you'll realise that the journey you've been on was all for the best".

"I don't know about that. Going to prison was definitely the worst part of it all. I don't see how that was for the best! I know that I was only inside for a few weeks but I hated every minute of it. Seriously, don't ever go there! It's mind-bumblingly depressing. You've got nothing to do but, y'know, sit and *think* about things. It was horrible".

"Well I wasn't exactly considering it as a future option!" Lottie scoffed, aghast at the bafflingly unnecessary cautionary tale. She hesitated again, still quite unable to fully resolve how she felt about her new fake fiancé. She just couldn't decide if she felt sorry for the unfortunate soul coming to terms with his own disastrous downfall, as though he was just yet another victim of society's chew-them-up-and-spit-them-out attitude towards their disposable celebrity idols, or if she simply wanted to slap the beautiful moron who had been blessed with so much in life and still considered having to "think about things" as being the worst consequence he had faced throughout his fall from grace. Although she didn't know it yet, Lottie would finally make her mind up about him in less than two minutes' time.

"Surely there must be something else you're good at?"

"Nope, nothin'".

"Well maybe now is the time to find something. There are lots of great adult education classes, and I'm sure if you really make the effort to – "

"Look, I already know that I'm not exactly the sharpest bulb in the tree. I don't need no adult education class to remind me of that! I'm really not very good any *anything* else", Roger candidly interjected, mixing rare melancholic humility with his usual brand of barefaced raw honesty. "I was terrible in school, absolutely terrible. I couldn't seem to understand even the simplest things no matter how hard I tried. Teachers were always calling my parents into school for meetings to discuss what was wrong with me, and the other kids would pick on me for being stupid. I failed every exam I ever sat. My Dad in particular would become so frustrated with me. I starting getting bullied and I hated it. But that all changed when I was around ten years old. I started playing football, and finally found that I could be *good* at something".

To Lottie's frustration, Roger's poignant trip down memory lane was interrupted by the restaurant manager's sudden appearance in the kitchen, to advise them that the paparazzi photographers they had all been waiting for had finally arrived outside.

"Just give us a minute!" she barked at him irately, without taking her eyes off Roger. "Sorry, I mean we'll come outside in just a moment. Thank you!" she added in a friendlier and much more approachable tone as she immediately realised how uncharacteristically rude she had been, while the offended manager stomped outside to place Lottie and Roger's food on the table for them. He reasoned that nobody was interested in the actual food or the restaurant, so normal service etiquette really didn't need to apply today. He muttered something foul about spoiled celebrities under his breath, and then disappeared back inside again while the photographers waited impatiently for their subjects.

"See, it's important to understand that football changed everything for me", Roger continued thoughtfully. "It was the first time I could ever do something and not be mocked for it. I was bloody good and it didn't take long for people to notice. My Dad signed me up for a local team, and that summer we went on to win the first tournament I ever played in. I even got given the Man Of The Match trophy, too! I remember that I was so shocked by that. I'd never won anything before then, you see. That was probably the best day of my life. Even to this day, everywhere I've ever lived or travelled since then, I've always brought that little trophy with me, like it's my lucky charm or something. I guess you think that's pretty stupid".

"Not at all!" Lottie enthused, with absolute sincerity. She was finally seeing a rare glimpse of the real human side to Roger that was far removed from the scandalous tabloid fodder that typically defined him, and she was beginning to like what she saw.

"My Dad was so proud of me that day", Roger continued nostalgically, with a misty-eyed smile emerging subtly on his handsome face. "In fact, I even got myself a little girlfriend later that day too, my first one. I guess I suddenly didn't seem like such a loser to the other kids anymore. There was a little party for the winning team at the local Youth Club, and my new girlfriend and me even had our first kiss that night. Which, of course, brings me to the only *other* thing I'm good at..."

Roger flashed Lottie a cheeky little wink, and she responded with an exaggerated eye roll. "Okay, okay", she laughed, playfully punching his arm. "Let's not ruin it! Come on, I think we should go outside and get these paparazzi photos done before they all leave".

Less than five minutes later, just two metres in front of almost a dozen paparazzi photographers and a frenzy of camera flashes, 'engaged' couple Lottie and Roger finally shared their very first kiss.

It was a surprisingly beautiful, tender moment of cynically contrived fakery.

Chapter Fifteen

"You're cheating on me? *You're* cheating on me! You're cheating on *me*!?"
Lottie repeated the words over and over, each time adding more inflection and sounding more and more dumbstruck with every repetition. There was a sharp edge of hysteria to her voice and an expression of hurt in her eyes; fragments of anguish and betrayal flashed across her maddened face, all but hidden behind a genuine surface of deep-seated fury. There could be no mistaking the shock and heartbreak that she was experiencing in that very moment.
Eventually, Lottie's outpouring of distress was interrupted as Roger called out from bathroom in a much more casual tone, "Lottie? What on earth are you doing out there?"
"Oh... nothing. Just practising for tonight", Lottie cheerfully called back, her angst-ridden face suddenly returning to its much more normal expression of gormless hopeful charm.

It was already promising to be quite a hot summer, and this was a particularly warm evening with barely a cloud in the sky. Roger and Lottie had arrived earlier that day to their suite at the Vaes House Hotel, a plush five-star resort in the centre of London that was hosting the launch of a hotly anticipated – at least according to its press release - fashion collection called "Pea P!" by designer Ninu Pea Pitchinu, and the two of them were using the room to dress and prepare themselves for the highly publicised event. There would be a red carpet, lots of photographers, lots of drinks, lots of guests – and an unforgettably explosive argument between one newly engaged celebrity couple that, if properly executed, would have people talking for weeks!

Roger was enjoying a nice long soak in the suite's enormous spa bath while Lottie was in the bedroom area, standing in front of the floor length mirror and rehearsing exactly what she was going to say when she confronted Roger later that evening. She was giddy and excited. She could hardly wait. In her mind's eye, she could already see all the headlines, the photographs and the attention she would receive after the showdown. She had to play it perfectly. She wanted to be seen as the wronged woman who had refused to be a victim; a fiery woman scorned who vehemently refused to allow any man to make a fool of her. She could envision herself becoming some kind of heroine for the modern tabloid age, and rather fancifully began to imagine herself as a positive role model for all the betrayed women out there by showing them exactly how a strong woman could and *should* kick her cheating man to the kerb. The fact that a helpful executive editor for some tacky tabloid magazine had premeditated the entire debacle did nothing to quell Lottie's elaborate flights of self-serving fancy.

This felt like it had been a long time coming, although

Lottie had been anticipating this day for so long now that part of her just couldn't wait until it was all over.

"You know, it's kind of going to be a shame when this engagement thing is finished", Roger suddenly called out from the bathroom, seemingly reading her mind and finally taking a very welcome break from the crude football chants he had been singing loudly all afternoon. "I know it's all part of the plan, but I just realised that it means we won't really get to see each other again after we break up tonight".

"I guess not", Lottie called back uncertainly. "But as you said, it's all part of the plan. Anyway, stop talking to me now. I need to concentrate. I don't want there to be any slip-ups tonight. This argument *has* to go *perfectly*!"

"You know, you should have been an actress!" Roger laughed, before returning to a rousing chorus of *'Who's That Wanker In The Red?'*, while Lottie turned back to face her reflection in the mirror and continued rehearsing exactly how she was going to confront Roger later that evening. David had told Lottie and Roger to stage their argument in the middle of the party at midnight. He had been very clear about that. She checked the time. It was now quarter past seven.

"We're engaged and you're cheating on me already? I'll kill you! *I'll* kill *you*!! I'll *kill* you!!!" she screamed enthusiastically at her red-faced reflection.

....

Less than a mile away, somebody else was very calmly awaiting the night's events with eager anticipation. He glanced at his wristwatch. Quarter past seven. The feeling also began to occur to him that this had been a long time coming. Today was finally the day, tonight would finally be the night and once it was all over with, there could be no going back. David tried to think of what he might have forgotten. He searched his brain for some little detail that he might have overlooked, something he would later come to regret, or an element of doubt or uncertainty in his mind. He continued to search. There was nothing.

He already knew this anyway.

He would undoubtedly soon have his exclusive story for *Celebs Today*, and owing to the fact that he had fiendishly orchestrated and arranged the whole sordid sham from the very beginning, his supposed journalistic intuition would appear to be unrivalled. *Celebs Today* would surely become the hottest selling tabloid magazine in the UK, and it would be all thanks to him.

Ashton Cain could never have covered such a story with the same accuracy, because he never would have had the gumption to make it happen in the first place.

Still, if everything went according to the plan, then by the end he would have so much more than a simple metaphorical feather in his cap from his current boss, who had never really valued or seen the true worth in David to begin with.

He had expected to feel more excited. He had expected to feel quite anxious or even nervous. But he didn't. He felt no emotion. He just felt in control for once.

....

Ashton Cain was also currently in the Vaes House Hotel with his new secret beau Angelica. Like Lottie and Roger, Ashton and Angelica were also preparing to go to the launch of "Pea P!" and had checked into a private suite earlier that afternoon. Angelica and Ashton had only been seeing each other for a few weeks, but since she was still in the process of divorcing her husband David, she had been quite insistent on keeping their relationship under wraps. This was the first time that she had even agreed to go somewhere public with him; it was purely an exercise in publicity for Ashton, who was hoping to make some connections to the fashion industry as part of his recent bid to enter into the world of professional modelling.

Angelica had agreed to attend the event with Ashton only because it was exactly what she wanted to do and this was exactly how she operated - but even so, she still had a few conditions for her new secret boyfriend.

"Don't hold my hand when we're in public", she sternly warned him. "Don't kiss me, don't open doors for me, don't refer to me as your partner or girlfriend or any other wretch-inducing label like that. Remember that we're here just so that you can make connections and be photographed looking handsome next to some famous faces. People like looking at models and also like to imagine that they're single and accessible, so that's exactly what you're going to tell them you are".

Ashton said that he understood, and he paused for a moment to lovingly admire his new girlfriend's matter-of-fact way of speaking and her no-nonsense approach to life in general. Angelica, meanwhile, sat down by the window and began skimming through a couple of tabloid magazines she had picked up from the hotel lobby.

"Are you looking at paparazzi photos of that dumb footballer again? If I were the jealous type, I might think you have a crush on him or something. Should I be worried? Ha ha..." Ashton very casually joked.

"I think you should change your shirt. The colour is clashing with my manicure".

"Right. So, I've got nothing to worry about, right?" Ashton jokingly asked, trying his best to emphasise what a casual, breezy question this was. He was beginning to feel a little insecure. His new lover was a very difficult woman to read.

"Yes! Your shirt! Change it…"

....

"Are you nearly ready yet?"
"Not quite! *This* stupid buggery dress won't zip up either! I think the size label must be wrong".
"Okay. Are you sure it wasn't shrunk in the washing machine like the last couple of dresses you tried on?"
"Yes! What time is it now?"
"It's almost ten o'clock. Do you want me to come and help zip you into your dress?"
"*No!*"
"Alright then. Shall I just wait out here while you shout at your clothes some more?"
"*Yes!!!*"

Thirty minutes later, Lottie finally had managed to wrestle herself back into what was actually the first dress she had tried on almost two hours prior, and she

205

had finally achieved some kind of uneasy alliance with her own reflection. She wasn't feeling *quite* as thin and fabulous as she had hoped she would be at this point in time, but after several hours of arduous preparation she finally accepted her appearance with moderate satisfaction. Roger rather sweetly kept telling Lottie great big whopping lies about how amazing she looked, and although she didn't really believe him, she was certainly beginning to appreciate his efforts.

After several hours of Lottie dressing, styling her hair and applying her makeup – plus the ninety whole seconds it took Roger to put on a designer shirt and choose a pair of trousers - celebdom's newest fake couple finally made their way downstairs to the main event of Ninu Pea Pitchinu's fashion line launch. Their first port of call was to the large reception area where the photographers were waiting to take pictures of all the celebrity guests with Ninu, in front of a large "Pea P!" graphic that had been set up to advertise her latest collection. It was taking some time for all of the guests to pose for their photographs and there were already a few people waiting ahead of Lottie and Roger when they arrived, so they had to linger for a little while until it was their turn. This gave Lottie a much-needed chance to discuss something with Roger that had been bothering her all evening.

"Listen, before we meet Ninu, I want you to *really* concentrate on how you're pronouncing her name.

Apparently, she's a little sensitive about it and always thinks that people are making fun of her. Believe me, it's not always nice when people get your name wrong".

Roger obliged and practised a couple of times. Each attempt at pronouncing her name seemed to be more hopelessly, awfully and irredeemably wrong than the last. This already had enormous potential for embarrassment.

"Okay, forget about *her* name for a moment. I'll just introduce us both, and you just try to avoid calling her by her name. But let's at least practise the name of the collection. There's just something I can't quite put my finger on about the way that you're pronouncing it that's possibly going to irritate her".

"Pee-Pee?"
"No, it's 'Pea P!'"
"*Pee*-Pee!"
"No, you're supposed to pronounce the 'ah' sound. Like '*Pey-ah, Pey*'. Understand?"
"Okay, I've got it! '*PEE-PEEEE!!!*', right?"
"I'll do the talking".

Eventually it was their turn. Ninu greeted Lottie and Roger warmly, and chatted with Lottie a little about her collection while two of the official photographers had another minor squabble about the lighting. Roger had simply decided not to speak. He would be far less likely to get into trouble that way, he reasoned.

"I wanted this collection to be about inclusion and equality", Ninu enthusiastically explained to Lottie. "I wanted to bring the city together, for people from all walks of life. Given my heritage and place of birth, I know what it's like to be marginalised and to feel like an outsider while living in London".
"Where are you from?" Lottie asked, genuinely curious.
"Hull", came the unexpected response, while Ninu's deadpan expression dared anyone to so much as comment on this.

After a little time, the photographers appeared to reach an agreement about the lighting, and finally began taking pictures again. Lottie and Roger posed for a few photographs with Ninu, and then posed for some more pictures with just each other. They hugged each other and staged a couple playful romantic poses and over-the-top kisses. Their romance might have been as fake as a three quid note, but the natural exhibitionist inside each of them helped Lottie and Roger to fully embrace the theatrics of their performance.

Lottie and Roger continued to pose, hug, laugh and kiss for the cameras until they had entirely exhausted their welcome and the photographers finally had to ask them to leave. They took their complimentary champagne and - since it was already now quarter to eleven - they found their seats inside the main hall ready for the runway show to begin.

....

David entered the house with surprising ease. He hadn't been too concerned about this part. He had a Plan B prepared for gaining access nonetheless – there was always a meticulously prepared Plan B, C and D for a man like David - but since he had entered the property without any difficulties on his first attempt, he had a little time to walk around the place and inspect the surroundings. He was very careful not to touch anything.

The house was almost exactly as he had expected it to be. It somehow felt both cold and flashy at the same time. The minimalistic modern décor chosen by its current occupant was at complete odds with the sporadic vulgar flashes of tacky opulence; gaudy over-the-top furnishings appeared scattered haphazardly around the place, providing a harsh, ugly contrast to the otherwise sparse rooms. It was an ostentatious eyesore from top to bottom in David's opinion. None of this came as a surprise to him. But he wasn't there to judge the interior decoration after all. He had something much more important in mind. He crept around the lifeless house with extreme care and caution, and his gentle footsteps echoed softly off the polished marble.

He crept upstairs and one particular object on display caught his eye. He picked it up, went into the bedroom and waited. It had only just gone past eleven o'clock. There was some time to kill.
David tried to think of some little detail that he might have overlooked, something he would later come to regret, or an element of doubt or uncertainty in his mind. There was nothing.

He already knew this anyway.

....

"What time is it now?"
"It's almost twenty past eleven already. I hope they start the event soon. We're supposed to break up at midnight!"

Lottie and Roger were seated two rows up from the catwalk. Lottie had tried and failed to acquire front row seats for the two of them where they could be more visible as guests, but they had at least managed to be seated close to the stage at the front of the catwalk, so she was happily satisfied that her face would appear in a lot of the photos behind the models. Finally, after a thirty-five-minute delay, the lights dimmed and the host for the evening came onto the stage to introduce Ninu. Lottie groaned inwardly as she realised that the celebrity host for the evening was Mrs O – the still-currently-suspended presenter of *Women's Natter* who had inadvertently humiliated Lottie on national TV all that time ago.

Mrs O introduced Ninu Pea Pitchinu without any major slipups or humiliation, somehow managing to pronounce her unusual name perfectly, despite this being the same woman who had failed so spectacularly at saying a simple three-syllable moniker like 'Lottie Klünt', and then Ninu launched straight into her slightly bonkers, self-serving speech about what exactly had inspired her fashion collection, 'Pea P!'.

"'*Pea P!*' is a collection that evokes a feeling of a circus train with an explosive natural disaster backdrop to it; shiny and with subtle undertones of the number '0' emitting from a bold new place with lots of linear lines, but not too straight, and lots of boxes but sort of circular, with a suggestion of brown but not the actual colour brown. Basically, I set out to create something with this fashion line that embodies a suggestion of being, has an apocalyptic feel but is still very grounded; a sort of abstract realism from a central feeling of nothingness", she passionately twittered to her baffled but eager audience. Then the show lights came on, the music boomed and the models began walking up and down the catwalk, each of them wearing nothing more than a simple oversized white T-shirt that in Lottie's opinion looked almost indistinguishable from the last one.

Finding herself losing interest after less than a minute, Lottie began to nonchalantly glance around the audience to see who else was at the event watching the show. She bit her lip when she saw her rival reality TV star Stefani Summerstone jumping up and down in her seat in feigned, attention-grabbing excitement, but she did feel a twinge of guilty secret satisfaction when she realised that nobody else appeared to be paying her any attention at all despite all the effort, and that the latter stages of her latest pregnancy had made Stefani's weight balloon in such a drastic way that Lottie *knew* she must be loathing. She also saw her ex-agent Teddy sitting somewhere in the back and casually reading a newspaper instead of watching the actual show. He wasn't even pretending to be interested. He was probably only there to source new clients, Lottie quickly realised. She remembered that she herself had met him at such an event years before. He felt her eyes on him, looked up, smiled and waved at her. Thankfully, he had never been the type of person who had enough patience or enough interest to bother holding on to a grudge.

Lottie also noticed Roger's ex-wife Cherlene sitting in an

opposite row and pouting vainly towards the cameras, clearly more wrapped up in her own appearance than anything that was occurring on the catwalk. Being famous seemed to have changed her whole persona almost overnight. The very notion of celebrity could so often have that effect on people. Even after all these years, it was amazing to Lottie how just a few magazine and television appearances offered to one moderately well-known ex-WAG had suddenly left the woman feeling as though she was the greatest, brightest star that the whole universe revolved around, or at least that's what Cherlene's vain outward appearance now seemed to be suggesting.

Cherlene didn't appear to have noticed Lottie and Roger, nor did Roger seem to have noticed her. Lottie glanced sideways at him. He was looking in the opposite direction, having just recognised Angelica Paige and the new handsome companion who was accompanying her.

Roger turned away from Angelica once she noticed him staring and turned his attentions back to Lottie. It was now just twenty minutes to midnight and the fashion show was drawing to a close. "Are you really sure you want to go through with this? There's no going back once we start", he discreetly asked Lottie, subtly gesturing towards the time displayed on his wristwatch. "Of course I'm sure! What are you suggesting? That we forget about breaking up, keep the phoney engagement going and *actually* get married?" Lottie laughed.

213

"Ha ha – can you imagine what David would say to that?"
"It would certainly be ironic, wouldn't it? We enter into this fake engagement just so we can have an attention-grabbing breakup for the publicity of it, but it ends up like a fairy tale where we get married and give up on being famous altogether. We could run away to the country together, buy a house near my parents and live out the rest of our days in blissful obscurity!"

They both thought intently about it for a moment.

"It'd probably make a nice cheesy romantic ending for a *book* or something, but real life never has such clichéd endings!" Lottie shrugged dismissively, and Roger completely agreed with her, still quite amused at the ridiculousness of the idea.

The fashion show finished. Ninu and the models stood graciously on the stage for a few minutes to receive their applause and greedily soak in all the attention, and then the guests made their way to the large and exclusive bar area of the hotel that was being used for the after party, which – although nobody ever admitted to this - was the real reason that most of the guests were ever even at these events in the first place. There also appeared to be invited photographers just about everywhere to capture the action, which was the other significant reason why most of the guests were there.
Lottie and Roger ordered several large cocktails each. Lottie drank hers quickly because she was feeling

incredibly nervous, and Roger drank his quickly because he quite liked drinking large drinks. After a few minutes, Lottie was relieved to observe that Roger had attracted the attentions of a couple of wannabe models, although they were cautiously keeping their distance from him while his supposed fiancé was there. This was exactly what they had been counting on.

"Roger, listen to me carefully. I'm going to go to the bathroom now, and when I come back, we'll start this thing", Lottie very discreetly whispered to Roger, casually glancing around the room and deliberately facing away from him. She was speaking so discreetly that not only would any potential casual observer be unable to tell what she had said; they probably wouldn't have even detected that she had said anything to him at all.
He very subtly nodded in inconspicuous agreement, the cloak-and-dagger effect of which was rather spoiled when he smiled and loudly concurred, "Okay! I'm ready! Let's *do* it!"
Nonetheless, Lottie disappeared into the bathroom and pretended not to notice the two pretty young girls who seemed as though they were quite interested in intimately acquainting themselves with her handsome fake fiancé as soon as the opportunity presented itself. Despite there being no one else in the lavatories, Lottie still nervously hid in the cubicle for a few minutes as she mentally prepared herself for the upcoming confrontation. After all this time and all the effort that

they had put in leading to this moment, she knew that she had to make this as explosive and dramatic as possible.

She exited the stall and checked her watch. It was midnight. An idea struck her that there was one last thing she could do to prepare for this performance. She took out the lemon slice from her drink that she had left on the vanity unit and rubbed it under her eyes; the effect of this made her eyes turn red and watery, and made her heavy makeup run ever so slightly down her cheek. It was a sneaky little trick that she had remembered Stefani Summerstone doing after they had appeared on the *Women's Natter* show together to make herself look as though she was in tears. She looked in the mirror again. It really did appear as though she had been crying.

'*This is it*', Lottie thought to herself, as she stared intently at her tearful, puffy-faced reflection in the mirror, '*By tomorrow morning, you're going to be the most talked about woman in Britain*'.

Lottie rushed out of the bathroom with her head down and her hair largely covering her eyes so that no one would see her fake tears yet. Nobody paid her any attention at all. She rushed over to Roger as quickly as she could, but then hesitated suddenly. Something had gone wrong. The original plan was that Roger was *supposed* to have found someone – quite literally anyone

- to flirt with so as to give Lottie the chance to 'catch' him in the act, and this would be the catalyst to launch their spectacular public fight, but he hadn't. For some reason, he was just standing alone under the bright light of one of the overhanging chandeliers where Lottie had left him. Her mind raced with confusion. Had he forgotten what he was supposed to do already? Had he simply not been able to find anyone to converse and flirt a little bit with? Had he changed his mind? After the unexpected moment of hesitation, Lottie made the hasty decision to just stick with the original script as planned and to confront him exactly as she had rehearsed, with just a little last-minute editing.

"*ROGER SCOTT!!*" she bellowed across the room with all her might, "I've... erm, I've just *spoken* to your little tart in the bathroom. We're *engaged* and you're *cheating on me* already!?? Did you think you would get away with it!? I'm gonna *kill* you!!!"

Chapter Sixteen

The music continued to play, but nobody was listening or dancing anymore. The room had fallen into an abrupt shocked silence. Lottie was panting heavily. She looked upon her fiancé with her maddened red eyes, and he looked back at her with open-mouthed awe.

'This is going brilliantly!' Lottie thought to herself, her thoughts racing a mile a minute, *'I've got absolutely everybody's attention, and they're hanging off my every word!'*

"Haven't you got anything to say for yourself? Did you think I wouldn't find out!? Did you *think* I was the type of girl who would just *put up* with you *cheating* on me!!?" she screamed at the fake fiancé she was accusing of infidelity. Roger said nothing, just as he had been instructed. The wide-eyed expression of alarm on his face was doing all the talking for him. Lottie's hysterical reaction was saying the rest.

Although she tried to focus and just concentrate on the moment, Lottie could feel herself becoming submerged to the point of drowning in the attention and it was fantastic. The awareness of it all was almost euphoric. Her every sense was on fire. She could almost physically *sense* all the eyes on her; people were genuinely fascinated for the first time in a long time to see what

219

she was going to do next and to hear what she was going to say next. More than that, they seemed to be finally recognising that she existed again. Like long-forgotten caveman taking the time to leave his handprint on the surface of the world, this was Lottie's moment to make her mark and feel as though she was on the world's stage once again.

Lottie continued to scream and rant some more at the top of her lungs, and pretended not to notice that some of the party guests that surrounded her had now taken out their mobile phones to record the commotion. Most of the official photographers delicately refrained from taking photos – they had only been hired by Ninu's management to take promotional pictures after all – but one or two of them still couldn't resist the opportunity to snap the drama as it unfolded in front of them. It didn't matter too much at this point. There would be no shortage of juicy photos before the night was over with; whatever happened now was simply a precursor to the excitement of the headline-grabbing police drama that was planned for later on at Roger's house.

Roger stared at Lottie waiting for his cue, and very subtly his eyes darted towards the exit. Lottie nodded ever so slightly at him. This was his signal to leave. "I'm so sorry", he meekly uttered as he turned on his heel and fled out the door, straight to the valet station to retrieve his car. Moments later, he had sped off into the night, leaving his broken-hearted fiancé all alone in the centre of the busy party, with hundreds of eyes all fixed entirely on her.

Under the harsh glare of the overhanging light fixture, Lottie stood motionless for dramatic effect and wailed loudly. This was quite literally her moment in the spotlight. She cried and held her head in her hands. She appeared to be utterly devastated, and the shell-shocked party-goers that surrounded her waited uneasily to see what she was going to do next. Nobody could have possibly guessed just how much Lottie was actually enjoying herself in this moment.

Eventually, after the dramatic pause had been fully exhausted, one or two people cautiously approached Lottie to comfort her, but Lottie wasn't quite ready to share the spotlight just yet. Even Lottie's reality TV rival Stefani Summerstone made a determined effort to join in on the drama by loudly stammering, "You should drop that no-good loser like a done. You're dunning, darlin', you don't need no man. Drong women like us should dick together!" but Lottie didn't even bother to acknowledge Stefani's obvious attempt to latch onto the excitement, nor the ridiculous feigned speech impediment that she was apparently still clinging to.

She snapped out of her pitiful fake crying and moved on to the next part of her well-rehearsed performance. *This* was her time to shine. *This* was her moment to define herself in the public eye. Lottie almost felt as though she could sense her future self nostalgically and proudly watching this very moment through the window of her memories, as she loudly announced to the whole world in general, "I am *not* going to let him get away with this! I am *not* going to let him leave me here like this! Somebody, call me a taxi!.."

If this were a movie, this would have been a perfect climactic moment of high drama. Unfortunately, moments like this are often ruined by real life; in this instance, Lottie's emotive display was spoiled by a wannabe comedian in the crowd who loudly yelled his sarcastic response, "*You're a taxi!*"

Lottie flashed the man a brief yet severely cold icy stare for a split second, but then immediately continued her rant, expertly sidestepping the irritating interruption as though it hadn't even occurred.

"I'm going home to confront my no-good fiancé! He's going to regret two-timing a woman like me. He'll never cheat on another woman again if it's the last thing I do. *Lottie Klünt* will *not* be made a fool of!"
With that bold statement, Lottie left the party and stormed outside, radiating confidence, determination and the ballsy demeanour of a fiery woman scorned, to a nearby taxi rank across the street from the hotel. Her dress billowed behind her, almost unable to keep up with her purposeful gait. Her hair whipped against her shoulders with every determined stride. She couldn't

remember when had she last felt this confident and sure of herself. Maybe she should have been an actress after all, she mused, as she jumped into a nearby taxi and instructed the driver to take her to Roger's address. Maybe she would even be offered some gigs once her profile had been raised by all of this. Perhaps she would be offered an autobiography deal, or even have her likeness made into a waxwork figure in the Madame Tussaunds museum or something. She would *definitely* lose some weight first, she firmly decided, privately wondering just how much wax it would actually take to preserve her voluptuous posterior for posterity.

"So, how was the party at the hotel? There were a lot of cars and photographers outside. Must've been a big deal. I bet it was nice mingling with all those famous people", the taxi driver piped up conversationally, in an attempt to distract Lottie from the fact he had just inadvertently taken what would turn out to be a fairly costly wrong turn.
"Oh, it was interesting…" Lottie shrugged vaguely, still distantly preoccupied by her rather ambitious daydreaming.
"I was hoping I'd get to meet a few gorgeous fashion model-types leaving the hotel tonight, but sadly I haven't seen any yet".
The taxi driver suddenly felt the glare of Lottie's full attention as her eyes bore mercilessly into the back of his skull. She said nothing, very pointedly.
"No offense intended to you, love", he quickly

stammered, backpedalling. "I mean, we all come in different shapes and sizes, don't we? Hey, didn't you just get engaged to some famous footballer or something?"

"Roger Scott, yes", Lottie responded coldly, "But let's just say that after tonight, he'll be out of my life for good. I'm sure you'll read all about it tomorrow. No-one insults Lottie Klünt's honour and gets away with it!" she added ominously.

"Right, right. Good for you! That's the spirit", he responded encouragingly, before politely enquiring, "Who is Lottie Klünt?"

Ten minutes later, Lottie arrived at Roger's house. There was a rather sizable crowd of photographers already waiting outside the house when her taxi pulled up. Word had quickly spread after Lottie and Roger's public bust up at the hotel, and Lottie's repeated declaration that she was going home to confront him had guaranteed that several paparazzi groups quickly rushed over to Roger's house to witness whatever was going to happen before she had even arrived. Some were casually smoking cigarettes, some were sitting in cars listening to the radio, some were chatting on their phones, but as soon as Lottie stepped out of the vehicle they stepped into action, blinding her in a maddened blaze of camera flashes.

Staring ahead and pretending to ignore the frantic rabble of the dozen or so paparazzi photographers, Lottie's face demonstrated her most ferocious expression of fury, just as she had been practising all afternoon. She stormed to the front door, let herself into Roger's house with the electronic key she had been given earlier and then slammed the door shut behind her. For the first time all day, Lottie was met with complete stony silence. She embraced the moment, resting the back of her head against the door and breathing a sigh of relief. The hardest part was almost over. Now, she and Roger just needed to pretend to have a noisy altercation at home that was loud enough to warrant a headline-grabbing police visit, to absolutely ensure that this would be a celebrity breakup that would be the top story on everyone's lips by tomorrow morning.

Still, the house was deathly silent.

....

A quick check reassuringly revealed that the home security alarm was still deactivated. It was already disabled when the intruder had arrived earlier that evening. Laughably, the mysterious figure hadn't even needed to use the electronic security key they had stolen weeks before. This was almost too easy.
The intruder heard a woman come in through the front entrance and decided to make a swift exit. All of the commotion and attention was focussed outside in the

street at the front of the house. The shadowy figure tiptoed unnoticed through the kitchen; cat-like footsteps, cushioned by the sterile foot protectors that were being worn over the carefully-chosen soft footwear, echoed very softly off the polished marble. The intruder slipped silently out of the back door and climbed effortlessly over the back fence as though they had never even been there.

The last phase of the plan had been executed perfectly. Everything would fall into place by itself from here on.

....

"Roger? Roger!? Hello? It's me, Lottie! Are you there? We did it! Where are you?"

Lottie wandered around the house, switching on lights and trying to make her presence known. After all the lights and the noise from the lively fashion show, the darkness and quiet of Roger's house came as something of a relief. Lottie's ears were still ringing from the loud music and chaos of the party. Her footsteps echoed loudly as she paced across the marble floor. Surely, Roger must be home already. He had left the hotel quite some time before she did, and the taxi driver had blatantly ripped her off with several unnecessary lengthy diversions. What could have taken Roger so long to arrive home? Peering discreetly out of a front window, Lottie recognised that Roger's favourite custom red roadster was parked in the short sweeping driveway – she had been altogether too distracted by the attentions of the photographers when she had arrived to have absorbed even the most obvious details about her surroundings - and she remembered that this was the car he had driven to the hotel in that night. Therefore, he was very clearly home.

Reasoning that Roger was likely upstairs taking a shower or changing his clothes, Lottie decided to help herself to a well-deserved glass of wine from the kitchen while she waited for him. She noticed a cutlery drawer that had been left open. The self-closing drawer shut itself with an unexpected, satisfying 'whoosh' noise as soon as Lottie pressed her fingers on it. The sleek kitchen was so painstakingly modern, futuristic and featureless in its design that it took a couple of minutes of rummaging through handle-less cupboards before Lottie found where the glasses were stored, and another minute before she found and identified the fridge. She poured herself a large drink and sat down in silence.

Although it didn't take her long to empty the wine glass, by the time she had finished she was already beginning to grow concerned by Roger's apparent absence.

"Are you there, Roger?" she eventually called out from the bottom of the staircase. "Did you see how many photographers were outside? Exciting, isn't it? Maybe we should have our argument by an open window so they can actually hear us, what do you think?"

Lottie began to tentatively walk up the flamboyant glass staircase that dominated the entrance hall. "We ought to hurry up and start before the police arrive. Who's making the anonymous call to the police, by the way? One of the paps? Roger? Hello?" Lottie called out loudly. There was still no response. It was starting to become somewhat unnerving.

Until now, Lottie had only briefly been inside Roger's house twice and had never had any reason to venture upstairs before; she tiptoed cautiously with an awkward sense of unease, almost feeling like an unwelcome trespasser in someone else's home.

Reaching the top of the stairs, Lottie opened the first door that she came to and called out Roger's name. It was an empty bedroom, probably a guest room as far as Lottie could tell by the lack of visible personal possessions. It slowly began to occur to her that the fake argument and her angry tirade had perhaps all been too personal for Roger, and that it was possible he had now changed his mind about the whole breakup plan. She began to wonder if she had been too harsh and insensitive with her faux-outrage, and began to hope that he hadn't been too upset by it all. Not everyone had the type of thick-skinned personality that could handle such public shame, especially just for the sake of a few more column inches in the fickle tabloids. She had only been thinking about herself and her own precious publicity until now, but now that she was alone and far away from all the excitement and encouragement, it all was beginning to feel rather selfish and superficial. Roger's ex-wife had been at the fashion show, Lottie now remembered. She hadn't noticed whether or not Cherlene had stayed for the after party and therefore witnessed Lottie verbally tearing Roger apart, but what if she had? The poor chap was probably completely humiliated.

Or maybe he had just fallen asleep.

Lottie cautiously pushed open the door of the next room and found that there was a single light on inside. *This* looked more like Roger's bedroom. There were clothes on the floor, pieces of men's jewellery on the cabinet, various framed newspaper stories illustrating Roger's former football glory days decorating the walls, numerous mirrors around the place, but no sign of Roger. The large unmade bed was definitely empty. Lottie was about to turn around and leave when a particular object caught her eye. A fairly large football trophy was lying haphazardly on the floor. Lottie walked across to the other side of the room and picked it up. It was heavy.

The trophy featured a surprisingly weighty gold plated football on top of a thick wooden pillar. Lottie read the inscription, "*Roger Scott. Man of the Match. Under-11's league, Brixton Juniors' Academy*". There appeared to be some hair stuck to the corner of the weighty base, and some dark red gloop...

... which was also on the floor, leading to the side of the bed...

... where Roger was lying lifelessly in a pool of his own blood, with a large kitchen knife protruding out of his back.

....

"What do you think?" one paparazzo asked, approaching two other photographers who were sitting idly on the kerb outside of Roger's house, "Shall we give it another half an hour and then go home? It's almost one thirty now, and it doesn't look like anything else is going to happen tonight".

As one, the three men stared up at the open bedroom window that was just visible from the street. Thick sculpted conifer trees in the garden covered the majority of the ground floor, so all that could be seen from the street was Roger's car in the open driveway and a single light on in what appeared to be an upstairs bedroom. One or two of the photographers had already given up and gone home for the evening. There certainly appeared to be nothing worth sticking for around to witness here.

Suddenly, the quiet street was shaken by the most horrific, spine-tingling scream that bellowed and echoed from the open window. A frenzy of lightbulb flashes lit up the dark night as all the photographers aimed their cameras at the house.

Moments later, a red-faced Lottie emerged from the front door and ran frantically into the street; there was a look of maddened panic on her face, her heavy eye makeup streamed down her cheeks, and she was brandishing what appeared to be a large knife in her hand.

Lottie froze abruptly under the sudden glare of the frenzied camera flashes.

"What the – ! Guys, is that a knife in her hand? Is that *blood*!?" one of the cameramen called out, as the alarmed group quickly began to notice the dark red substance that seemed to be dripping off the large blade that Lottie was still instinctively clutching.

The only other sound that could be heard was the distant siren of police cars already racing towards the house.

....

It was already now six o'clock in the morning. The custody sergeant tried and failed to stifle a large, hippopotamus-sized yawn as he stood outside the police interview room. It had been a long night already. Inside the room, officers were still interviewing a murder suspect, a woman named Lottie Klünt, who had been arrested hours before at the home of her very recently deceased fiancé. It wasn't going well. She had been making very little sense since the moment they had first brought her in. Her solicitor repeatedly urged her to remain silent. She wasn't taking his advice. It quickly occurred to the solicitor that things weren't looking too promising for him either, professionally speaking.

"No, I didn't say I was going to kill him!" Lottie almost shrieked, determinedly, "Well, yes technically I *did* say that, but I didn't mean… What? No, no he wasn't *actually* cheating on me. Yes, I made that part up, but… What? What? No, that was just an excuse for…. What? We weren't even engaged! I know we *said* that we were, but…"

"We've already got several videos and countless witnesses all contesting to the fact that yesterday evening, while drinking at the Vaes House Hotel, you threatened to kill your fiancé after discovering that he was cheating on you with another woman", the first officer repeated, in a calm monotone.

"You see, I didn't *mean* it literally… There really *wasn't* another woman! We just wanted people to think that – "

"He then ran away from you after the confrontation and fled home, you chased after him in a blind rage, and then an hour later he is found dead with a knife in his back and his head bashed in", the second officer repeated. "And you were the only other person in the house". There was a thinly-disguised trace of weariness and impatience in his voice. They had been going around in circles all night. Why wouldn't the woman just hurry up and *admit* what everyone already knew she had done!

"No, but… I wasn't actually *angry*. It was all part of the *plan* for me to follow him home! It wasn't a real chase.

He wasn't *actually* scared of me…"

"And what you're telling us is that even though you repeatedly said that you were going to kill your fiancé after accusing him of cheating on you, you actually *weren't* going to kill him, he *wasn't* cheating on you and now you're saying that he *wasn't* even your fiancé?"

"That's right", Lottie sat back triumphantly. She was just as shaken and confused by the night's events as anybody, and was clinging desperately to the deluded belief that the whole ordeal would soon be over once it became clear that this was all one big catastrophic misunderstanding. It had barely even begun to sink into her mind that Roger was really dead yet, much less how preposterous her cries of innocence actually sounded against the weight of suspicion around her. But the reality was slowly beginning to creep in, little by little, and the panic was very quickly rising…

"So, let's suppose for one moment that *any* of that was true", the first officer began, clearing his throat, "Who else do you think might have wanted to harm Roger Scott, the fiancé you're now saying you weren't really engaged to, while you were home alone with him and coincidentally just moments after you had announced that you were going to kill him?"

"Stefani! It was probably Stefani!" Lottie spluttered animatedly as she banged her fists on the table, simultaneously ignoring the surprisingly facetious tone of the police officer's question and her solicitor's near-frantic urging of her to remain silent. "Stefani Summerstone! We're not exactly the best of friends, and she hates anyone who becomes more famous than she is. She was at the fashion launch and the party… she heard everything I said to Roger. You don't understand what it's like for these desperate reality TV stars; they become so crazed and hungry by it all that by the end they'll do *anything* for attention and headlines!"

The two officers exchanged less-than-subtle glances at Lottie's ill-thought-out statement and her apparent bizarre belief that this damning assertion somehow didn't apply to herself. It was beginning to look to them as though she had completely lost her mind! Lottie's solicitor tried to request a break from the interview on behalf of his client, who seemed determined to keep on digging a deeper and deeper pit for herself, but there appeared to be no stopping Lottie right now. Her erratic train of thought suddenly took another wild and unexpected swerve. "No – wait! *Cherlene*! Roger's ex-wife! It must've been Cherlene! She was at the party too! I've heard that she was going mad with jealousy over our engagement. I bet *she* killed him to just stop us getting married!"

"I thought that you *weren't* going to get married?"

"Well, technically... yes. No. I mean, we said that we were going to get married, but we weren't *actually* going to get married. But Cherlene didn't know that. Oh – there was another woman too... An... An... Angie.... *Angelica*! That was her name. Roger mentioned her once, how she kept driving past his house and things after he broke up with her. She was secretly obsessed with him. At least, I think that she was! It could have been any number of people really. And I bet that this is just scratching the surface, I actually barely knew the man in reality. I'm sure you've read all about him, he probably upset loads of women with his cheating and so on. But not *me*, as I said just now. Forget what I said before. *That* was all lies".

"Then why did you say – ", the interviewer began to ask the obvious questions again, but he was interrupted as the last penny of realisation finally dropped in Lottie's mind. Suddenly, the hindsight of clarity presented itself, shining like a bright beacon in the thick murky fog of confusion and deception. With the power and momentum of a landslide, the grim reality of what had really happened to Roger all began to finally tumble into place. All of a sudden, it was all becoming painfully clear.

"*David*!!!" she screamed, "It was David! He must have been planning this all along! How on earth didn't I see this before now?"

By nine o'clock in the morning, Lottie had been formally charged with Roger Scott's murder. She was so hysterical by this point that a doctor had to be called to administer several strong sedatives just to calm her down, and it became clear to all concerned that a mental evaluation would be urgently required.

Alone in her cell, Lottie finally began to succumb to the tranquillisers, and she eventually drifted into a forced sedated sleep, hazily muttering and still repeating mindlessly, "Daaaavid... It was David... He must have planned it all along".

Chapter Seventeen

Three men sat wordlessly propping up the little bar as they drank small glasses of lager, and each quietly tried to concentrate on the tiny television set that was mounted to the wall. Despite the early hour, one of the men - a recent newcomer to town - had been there since the mid-morning and was quite clearly drunk already. He said nothing and seemed to be more preoccupied by the TV than anybody else. There was a simple entertainment news show being broadcast on the flickering screen, the presenters of which seemed to be enthusiastically engaged in a heated discussion about the latest news story occupying their headlines. The murder of a famous British ex-footballer.

"Excuse me. Do either of you chaps understand what they're saying?" the most well-dressed and most inebriated of the trio asked the other men after a while, indistinctly pointing towards the TV screen that engrossed him.
"Not a clue", the eldest of the men responded. "That's the only problem with living abroad, they don't show much English telly for some reason".

The well-dressed drunk, who had arrived alone and was a newcomer to the local expats in this particular bar, shrugged noncommittally and turned back to concentrate on the TV. The old man who had responded decided to take the opportunity for some much-needed conversation, and continued merrily, "Still, I wouldn't trade it for anything. This is certainly not a bad place to retire! I spent nearly thirty years working in UK power stations, doing repairs, maintenance and so on before I came here. Coal, mostly. It was bloody dangerous work, too. One of the most dangerous jobs you can have. Most people don't realise".

The younger, thinner man sitting next to him piped up cheerfully, "I worked in *pest control* for forty years, myself. Nothin' glamourous, but it was an honest family business started by my Grandad, bless 'im. Mind you, I can't say I miss it much. I passed it onto my son when I retired four years ago and I've never looked back. It's not a job for the faint-hearted, let me tell you! I've seen some truly disgusting things in my time! If only you knew! It'd be enough to make your blood curdle".

The newcomer smiled politely, hiccupped and wordlessly took another sip from his drink. The two other men looked at each other.

"So how about you, stranger?" the elder man enquired, still eagerly trying to make polite conversation with the troubled loner. "What's your story? You look a bit young to have retired, if you don't mind me saying so".

"I used to work with celebrities", Clive Maxwell eventually responded after a long, heavy pause. He spoke quietly and there was a very distinct and unexpected dark edge of bitterness in his voice; his glassy eyes stared ominously into the distance. He seemed haunted by something. A broken shell of a man. Roger Scott's murder had had a profound effect on him. Clive strongly suspected that there was a lot more to his late client's death than had been reported, and he was almost certain that there was no way he could prove any of his suspicions. He wasn't even sure *what* he actually suspected, if it came to it. His disturbed demeanour was only broken by the occasional noisy drunken hiccup. "They used to call me a *PR Guru*, whatever that means", he went on, sourly. "I used to believe it, too. I really did! It's all too easy to believe your own hype in this game. But I gave it all up recently. I... I... I just had to! The tabloid industry is no place for an honest man. People think that celebs control the media, but in reality, it's entirely the other way around! Those at the top control what we think we know about everything, and these so-called celebs are just the fifteen-minute causalities of an unstoppable machine! And it goes on and on. No matter how many people the industry chews up and spits out, there's always the next crop of wannabe stars waiting to take their turn. Trust me, the things I've seen would shock you, the things I know would horrify you, and the things I *think* I know but can't actually prove... frankly, I don't *want* to know! *They* write the headlines. *They* write the stories. *They* write what we think is real. Let's just say that the media is a powerful tool, far more powerful than you realise, and that as a job, being a celebrity is

241

more dangerous and disgusting than either of your former professions put together!"

As one, the three men turned back to the TV, quite unable to come up with an appropriate follow up to Clive's unexpected dark summery of working in celebrity public relations. He then finished his beer, wished the two men a pleasant afternoon, and then staggered off into the sunshine to continue drowning his sorrows elsewhere.

After a while, the younger of the two remaining men broke the relaxed silence as he remarked to his companion, "Celebrities, eh? It makes you wonder".

The old man shrugged indifferently.

"Still, I bet the hours weren't that bad. I had to get up at *five* o'clock in the morning for nearly forty years! *And* a rat once bit off part of my toe!"

Just a few minutes away, on the very same sun scorched street on the Costa del Sol, a small group of tourists sat lazily on wicker loungers outside a beachside bar and cheered raucously as the waiter set their eighth jug of Sangria on the table. It was Sunday. They had gone to the beach that morning to nurse their collective hangovers, and by early afternoon they had moved on to the protective shade of the nearby *Straw Donkey* bar to ease their blistering sunburn, where they got an early start working on the next day's inevitable hangover. The equally hung-over waiter's blank responses indicated that he didn't speak any English, but after some creative pointing and shouting, the group had managed to order the cheapest, largest drink on the menu and left the lone server to continue watching the latest new Spanish TV game show that was apparently enthralling him.

A small pile of notoriously scandalous British tabloid magazines one of the women had picked up in a local store was prompting an energetic discussion that engaged the intoxicated holidaymakers. To nobody's surprise, the headlines in each of them were dominated by the same story.

LOTTIE MAINTAINS HER INNOCENCE: HER BIZARRE THEORY EXPOSED

'CRAZED' KLÜNT TOLD ME SHE WOULD 'GET RID' OF HER CHEATING LOVER, TAXI DRIVER REVEALS

ROGER SCOTT'S DELUDED KILLER FIANCÉ STILL DENIES THEIR ENGAGEMENT IN COURT

The last headline on the pile simply read;
JURY UNAMINOUSLY FINDS LOTTIE KLÜNT <u>GUILTY</u> OF MURDER

....

Lottie tottered into the centre of the prison canteen and then hesitated, just as she always did. 'This is so stupid', she tried telling herself, 'You *have* to at least eat *something*!'

Feeling the weight of at least a dozen set of unfriendly eyes all intently fixed on her, Lottie meekly made her way to the front of the prison shop, where she purchased just two cereal bars with what little money was left on her meagre credit allowance. She had been skipping meals every day since she had been incarcerated, and some of the prison officers were already beginning to express concern by the amount of weight she had shed. But by the time Lottie had walked through the large communal space, she had already begun to lose her appetite again.

Lottie's recent court trial had been *big* news in the UK, and just about every man and his dog seemed to have an opinion about how crazy and deluded Lottie must have become, how ludicrous her defence story had sounded, and what kind of intense messed-up relationship could lead to such a gruesome crime of passion. The other inmates of the prison that Lottie would call home for the next few years were also no exception to this. There were even rumours floating around that some of the more unscrupulous tabloids were willing to pay quite a lot of money to anyone who could somehow acquire a photograph of Lottie in her custodial cell, which had prompted a recent renewed effort of stealthy determination by the prisoners to smuggle in mobile phones, digital cameras and other such contraband devices. There was at least one unauthorised biography of Lottie's life in the works that she was currently aware of, as well as talk of a made-for-TV movie that was supposedly loosely based on the now-infamous story of Lottie murdering Roger. An unfavourable docu-drama, depicting Lottie as a jealous crazed killer driven to the depths of insanity by her fiancé's philandering, had already aired on television the night before.

Although she tried to focus and just concentrate on the simple task at hand, Lottie could feel herself becoming submerged to the point of drowning in the attention... and it was horrible. There was no doubt in her mind that all her fellow prisoners were talking about her, in fact she could almost physically *sense* all the eyes on her, and she hated absolutely every torturous minute of it. She could only hope against the odds that once the novelty of being in the company of an infamous jailed celebrity wore off, her fellow inmates would simply somehow forget that she even existed. She could only hope.

Flinging the bland cereal bars into a bin on her way out without even attempting to take a bite, Lottie rushed back to the comforting solitude of her cell. She was alone again. She slumped heavily onto the hard, single bed, ignored the familiar returning pangs of hunger and began to while away the afternoon doing exactly what she had done every single day since her trial; she began to mentally obsess about the circumstances that had led to her lengthy, undeserved prison sentence in the first place.

Why had nobody believed her innocence? *How* had the press managed to get away with portraying her in such a negative - yet technically still legally defensible - light since Roger's death? *Why* had David framed her for the murder that she was now utterly convinced he had committed? And *how* had he convinced her to go along with it so readily, blindly and naively, while helping to secure her own demise with such eagerness along the way? How was it possible that the fake news had become more believable to the world than the reality behind it?

Lottie mostly knew the answers to these questions whichever way she looked at them. The tempting allure of the spotlight had rendered Lottie so blind to the pitfall she was being led into, and more than anything that precise realisation was an incredibly bitter pill to swallow. So blinded by the lights was she that she hadn't even been able to see the real world around her anymore. Any rational or concerned thought that she may have had over the past year had been completely lost in the echo of David's words in their first meeting together. "If you want to be really, *really* famous…"

Well she certainly was famous now. Like countless others before her, she had chased infamy at all costs. She felt like an insignificant little creature that hadn't been able to resist the hypnotic deadly glow of a bug zapper. But with the cold shower of hindsight, Lottie could see now how she hadn't just been framed, but she had been unwittingly complicit in her own demise all along – and all for the sake of some fleeting fame! It all just seemed so futile and pointless now. And yet a certain knowledge couldn't escape Lottie; she knew, with grim inevitability, that there were thousands of people out there still willing to do whatever it might take for the chance to grab their share of the spotlight. There was an endless stream of lambs happily dancing their way to the slaughterhouse. Perhaps there always had been.

She had technically achieved all that she had ever claimed to want to achieve from this; she was skinny and she was famous, and she now wanted nothing more than for it to all go away. Be careful what you wish for...

The one question she still couldn't answer was *why*. Why had David actually killed Roger? What would drive him to such lengths? There was absolutely no obvious motive as far as Lottie could see. The question ate away at her. It lingered perpetually at the forefront of her mind every waking hour. She even dreamed about it. She fixated on it, night and day, almost possessed by the question that she knew she would likely never have an answer to. Nobody else was interested in her crazy theory, to matter how much she protested. She felt like the only sane person in a world that had turned completely insane overnight. Maybe the tabloids were right. Maybe she really was mad after all.

As far as she knew, David had been dismissed as a suspect by police long ago after nothing more than a cursory interview in his office, despite her repeated protests. Lottie could finally see so clearly now how she had effectively been helping to frame *herself* for Roger's murder since the very moment she had pretended to be in a relationship with him. But why *Roger*? Why *kill* him? This couldn't *just* be about the headlines. That just simply didn't make any sense to her, and never would. What did David *really* have to gain from all of this?

Roger had been absolutely right about one thing, Lottie remembered. There was absolutely nothing to do in prison but sit and *think* about things...

And unfortunately Lottie now had a LONG time ahead of her to think!

....

Inside the busy offices of the *Celebs Today* magazine headquarters, the phones were ringing incessantly. Computer keyboards were clattering relentlessly. People were cursing and arguing either with each other, cursing and arguing with themselves or cursing and arguing with the odd rage-inducing memo or uncooperative piece of office technology. In short, it was business as normal – except that for this particular tabloid magazine, their business had been going exceptionally well lately.

Safely nestled away from all the hustle and bustle occurring just outside his door, David leaned forward in his large expensive new leather chair. It was possibly his favourite item in the fancy new office he had recently acquired, he decided. It was comfortable, it was stylish. The vintage premium bull hide that it featured had been chosen by him personally, and that wasn't the only beautiful leathery thing currently sat in David's office.

"So, Cherlene Scott", David smiled, before remembering himself. "Sorry, I mean Cherlene... Mononym?"
"That's right", she cheerfully responded, still woefully oblivious as to what a mononym actually was.
"That's your professional name now? Cherlene *Mononym*?" David asked, barely masking his perplexity and wondering if it was already too late to burst her bubble. Cherlene simply nodded proudly in agreement. "Well, anyway", he continued, "I understand that it's been a very difficult year for you, what with everything that has happened, but I must say that your public profile has really been raised by all of this. Now that poor Roger has been laid to rest and that awful Klünt woman is safely behind bars, hopefully receiving the professional psychological help that she so dearly needs, I think that this is now the time to be looking forward".

David paused for a moment. Cherlene's waxy blank expression and near-permanent pout revealed nothing.

"Which reminds me, congratulations on your new job", he persevered. "I saw the announcement this morning that you're officially the new host of *Women's Natter* now that Mrs O has finally been fired. Seems like a great excuse for a new interview with us. Then next month we'll have the guest fashion tips column with you – don't worry, I'll get someone else to write it for you – and then in February, *Celebs Today* will announce that you're our new celebrity Agony Aunt as a reoccurring monthly feature. Again, we'll get someone else to actually *write* it for you, so you don't have to worry about a thing".

"There is one thing – ", Cherlene tried interjecting, but David wasn't quite finished talking yet.

"I'm so glad that you came to see me all that time ago", he smiled. "I *told* you that I could make you famous".

"Yes, about that", Cherlene piped up. There was a bothersome nagging thought still playing on her mind. "Do you remember that first meeting between us? You remember that I told you I had hired a private detective, and then I came to you with all those photos that proved my husband, I mean… *Roger*, was cheating on me with all those different women?"

"Yes?" David responded, frowning. An edge of

uncertainty crept into his voice.

"And I gave you all the photos the private detective had taken? You remember? You paid me for them. You asked me for the detective's contact details. But then you never actually used the pictures of him in the magazine article about our separation, which I always thought was a bit curious, to be honest".

"Go on..." David cautiously prompted her. What did she *know*?

"It's just... well", she shrugged, "I was just wondering if you still had them? Turns out I've been offered one of those ghost-written autobiography whatsits. They want me to talk about my marriage and divorce and stuff, so I reckon those exclusive photos might bump up the price".

"Oh!" David exhaled, clasping his hands together and trying not to reveal his inner relief. "I'm afraid we no longer have those photos. The last Editor-in-Chief of *Celebs Today* didn't like the idea of publishing them, so he put them in the shredder. There was nothing I could do about it. Thankfully, I'm in charge of the magazine now. I am finally in complete control".

Cherlene thanked him profusely and left the office. David leaned back in his large wingback chair and smiled a happy, satisfied little smile. After a few minutes of doing nothing but quietly enjoying the moment, he opened a desk drawer and removed the false bottom, revealing a secret compartment that contained a small key. He then walked over to the safe, opened it and carefully removed a concealed metal panel at the back, which in turn revealed another tiny hidden compartment. Inside the second veiled slot was a single thin folder. David took the secret folder back to his desk and began to look through some of the photographs that it contained.

It had been a good few weeks for David. *Celebs Today's* circulation had almost doubled since the Lottie Klünt scandal, and now that Ashton Cain had left the magazine to pursue his dream of becoming a fashion model, David had finally been rewarded with the much-coveted Editor-in-Chief role. This was a long overdue change in fortunes, at least from David's viewpoint.

His divorce from Angelica had also at long last been finalised; the warring couple had been awarded their decree absolute that very morning. Their bitter divorce negotiations had started to run a lot more smoothly in recent weeks; for some reason, Angelica seemed to have lost focus lately, and so they had eventually managed to reach an uneasy agreement over the items and money they had been so passionately fighting over for all this time. Although in the end, it might actually cost Angelica a little more than she had anticipated, David thought to himself, almost amused at the thought. She had wanted to take what he wanted to have, but she had pushed him too far, until all he wanted was to do the same thing to her. It was always going to be a dangerous game to play, because she never would have guessed that David had worked out exactly *what* she really wanted to have, and he knew exactly how to take it.

David had always suspected that underneath the surface, he could be quite a treacherous person to tangle with, and so he had gradually learned to submit to life's injustices. But then life – and his wife - had simply pushed him too far and taken everything away from him, until all he had left was his dangerously devious mind.

On top of one pile on David's desk, there was also still a copy of *Celebs Today*'s biggest selling issue to date, which was a very recent in-depth look at Roger Scott's murder at the hands of his jilted fiancé, the now-infamous murderess Lottie Klünt. It caught his eye momentarily.

'What kind of intense toxic romance could drive a seemingly normal person to such emotional extremes that they would actually commit murder?', the tantalising article had questioned. David liked that particular line. It had been his own suggestion. He had felt quite proud when he had written it.

David turned his attentions back towards the photographs that he had so carefully kept hidden for all this time. They had been taken by a private eye hired by Cherlene, and given to him in their first meeting together, which seemed like a lifetime ago now. He remained transfixed on one photo in particular. It showed Roger, who was still married to Cherlene at the time, kissing one of his secret lovers, a woman named Angelica. Or to use her full name at that time, *Mrs Angelica Paige*. A busy woman, David mused, who had somehow found the time to make her husband David's life one long agony of matrimonial misery *and* was able to maintain a brazen love affair with Roger Scott, right under David's nose.

It had always been about control, power and capricious nastiness with Angelica, but she had truly met her counterpart in David. He had always secretly suspected that deep, deep down they were actually more alike one another than they had ever appeared to be on the surface. Even throughout the entirety of their messy divorce, Angelica had been playing a very shrewd and spiteful game of taking away things that she knew David loved and would miss. She had also woefully underestimated him, just as she always had done. Something she hadn't counted on was David figuring out the one thing that Angelica loved and would miss, and finding a way to take it from her. Forever.

Still, they had all moved on now. David had done what he had set out to do. Angelica had also seemingly moved on, and was still secretly dating –

– a call from David's assistant suddenly interrupted his train of thought. He transferred a call to David's office from some washed up reality TV star, who was apparently desperate to extend her fifteen minutes of fame and wanted all the tabloid exposure she could get.

"Stefani Summerstone! Lovely to hear from you again", David chirped in the friendliest voice he could find. "Are we on a secure line? You're sure? Good! Congratulations on the birth of your latest child. Don't worry about those unfortunate paparazzi photos of your baby weight gain. The media can be very cruel sometimes. Still, there's no such thing as bad press, as they say! On that note, I have an idea I'd like to propose to you, so let's set up a private meeting to discuss this right away. Stefani, how would you feel about getting a famous boyfriend? Just for publicity, you understand. It could be very lucrative if we play it right, and it certainly wouldn't have to be for long..."

David put his feet up on his enormous mahogany desk and smiled as on the other end of the phone, Stefani expressed her eagerness to do *anything* to maintain her time in the spotlight... *This* was the type of person that always made his job so much easier.

"Before we discuss any more, let me ask you a question", David continued. "How much do you know about an up-and-coming model called Ashton Cain?"

THE END.

www.jacetadams.com

Printed in Great Britain
by Amazon